I Hate His/Her Ex

I Hate His/Her Ex

Alex Cooper

Library of Congress Control Number:		2011962373
ISBN:	Hardcover	978-1-4691-3516-8
	Softcover	978-1-4691-3515-1
	Ebook	978-1-4691-3517-5

This book was printed in the United States of America.

To order additional copies of this book, contact:
Xlibris Corporation
0-800-644-6988
www.xlibrispublishing.co.uk
Orders@xlibrispublishing.co.uk
302861

CONTENTS

Understanding It All

'When it comes to love, you need not fall but rather surrender, surrender to the idea that you must love yourself before you can love another. You must absolutely trust yourself before you can absolutely trust another and most importantly you must accept your flaws before you can accept the flaws of another.' Philosophy: Falling in Love

Love makes us vulnerable. We risk being hurt. And when we are vulnerable, we open ourselves up to a whole heap of crazy emotions and insecurities. This is extremely common, and there are not many relationships that do not go through some kind of emotional turmoil caused by these feelings. The key is in working out how to handle these emotions and build a happy, secure, and trusting relationship with your partner without fear, hatred, and jealousy taking over.

'My ex . . .' is possibly one of the worst things you can hear your partner say. So you hate your partner's ex. Really hate them. Not just a little, a lot! Not just how they look or act or any other single thing. It's actually everything and for a very good reason, you think.

Or do you really? Is it possible to hate someone you don't even really know? What do you hate? The illusion that you have created? The reality is, you most likely just hate the fact that they are part of your partner's past. However, that doesn't take away from those deep-rooted feelings you have whenever their name is mentioned, or something occurs that reminds you of it all. Or basically, anything else that brings to your attention that lurking somewhere is the darkness of an abyss that you wish would disappear from all living memory.

I often used to wish that all exes should be put on an island somewhere from which they would magically just disappear into thin air—forever to be forgotten. It doesn't take long to work out though by that this means the majority of the population would instantly vanish, including me. So it left me to deal with a horrible thought. They are not going to go away. Even if they move thousands of miles away, they are always going to have existed. So the only thing there is to do is to deal with it. And in dealing with it, it is worthwhile spending a little amount of time figuring out the best way to remove them from your mind and thoughts on a permanent basis.

The first thing to do to understand all of this better is to work out where the feelings have come from. There is no denying that all of our partner's exes are going to have faults and things about them that we really don't like. But why are we letting it worry us so much? This isn't a person that we have ever had to or are ever likely to spend vast amounts of time with. So does it really matter if they have traits that we dislike or look terrible or behave in ways that we would never dream of? The real issue we have is that they were at some point significant in the lives of the person we are now with. Understanding ourselves, our partners, and the relationships between the past and the present (and the future) will help us gain balance and harmony. We will gain a rational and informed thought process rather than letting our minds run crazy with ridiculous thoughts that are most likely a million miles away from the truth.

Not only can these thought processes destroy our inner self, our self-esteem, and our day-to-day lives, but they can also have devastating effects on our relationship. By holding on to anger and hatred, we will harbour negative feelings that will not only make us feel terrible but will also have an effect on how we act and behave towards others. The sooner we work on releasing these feelings, the sooner we will notice a huge change in how we feel and how we treat others, especially our partners.

One of the hardest things about hating his ex is admitting it. Not just to ourselves, but if we mention it to our friends, partner, family, or work colleagues, they will just think we are a bunny boiler with serious jealousy problems. However, it is much more common than people realise. Not many people can honestly say they like the fact that their partner was in a relationship with someone before them. At some level, people generally have some negative feelings towards that person or the situation. And the best way to deal with this is to work out a way of dealing with those feelings so they don't become a daily problem, and if they have become a problem, how to dispense of them and live as much of an ex-free life as possible.

Not all exes are in the past. Some are larger-than-life figures that are still involved in your partner's life at some level. This is covered more later in the book so we can learn how to deal with the issues, then let the thoughts and feelings go so we can live a stress-free life without this other person having any effect whatsoever on how we feel day to day.

In cases where the ex is in the past, it really is a case of putting them out of your mind where very rarely, if ever, they are ever thought about again. If the person is in the present, the trick is to learn to work out the very best way to deal with this for you.

When we get into a relationship with someone special, we want to be the best for them, the very best. And putting this pressure on ourselves can end up making us feel and act our worst. It brings out all of our insecurities as we judge ourselves harshly, believing that they either have had someone better than us in the past or will get someone better in the future. We can focus too much on ourselves in a negative way, comparing ourselves and pulling ourselves to pieces, highlighting all our bad points and forgetting all the good. It is at this stage that our fears and insecurities can take over. The more we focus on them, the more real they become.

For example, if we constantly think about our partner's past relationships, we can foolishly torture ourselves by imagining how happy they must have been with that person and how perfect it all must have been. And the more we go down this road, the more real this will become to us. We can eventually come to a crazy conclusion that our partner was much happier before we came along, with someone from his past, and that we are not good enough for them! This then leads us to think that they are probably going to leave us or that they wish they had never met us. We begin to believe that they wish they were still with their ex or various other very irrational and very badly informed conclusions.

To begin with, that relationship from the past is now over, which suggests that the relationship obviously was not meant to be or they would still be together. And secondly, they are with you because they choose to be.

Nobody is forcing them to be in this relationship; they are in it of their own free will and at any time if they did not want to be with you, you can be pretty much guaranteed they would let you know and would leave. So while you cannot predict the future and there are no guarantees as to whether someone will stay or leave, what you can do is live happy and be carefree in the moment, enjoying your relationship and living life to the full. Your relationship is much more likely to succeed, and you will be living a life full of love and happiness instead of fear, anxiety, and worry.

When we understand ourselves better, we can start to change patterns of behaviour and alter the way we see and react to things. Learning to accept our negative traits and admit when we are wrong about something is essential so that we stop going around in circles, reliving and recreating the same mistakes and circumstances. We can look out for things that trigger our emotions and learn how to deal with those emotions when they do surface so we can avoid repeating the same negative reactions over and again.

We have to remember when reading this book that although this will give you an insight into understanding it all better and techniques to deal with this part of your life, ultimately the decision is yours. Regardless of any advice, or what anyone else says, the choice is always yours. You are in charge of your own life, and you are the only person that truly knows what makes you happy and what is best for you. If there is something or someone in your life that is having the opposite effect, then you must always do what is best for you and your relationships. Everyone has great ideas on how to live other people's lives, but not many people have this same advice for themselves. The most important thing to remember when making decisions is that they are rationally thought out and informed, using intuition and emotion and doing what feels right. We often put off decision making as we are scared of making the wrong one. Making no decision at all is a decision within itself.

THE PAST

As much as we sometimes wish that the past wasn't there, sadly it is one of the things that is entirely impossible to change. We all have a history, and spending time dwelling on it prevents you from being able to move forward. We are not capable of understanding our partner's past. All we see is an illusion of what we think happened. So there really is not much point in wasting time and energy going over it. The reality of what happened is barely possible for even the people involved to remember accurately, let alone someone else trying to work it out. So, basically, the fact is, we should never delve deeply into someone else's past i.e., our partner's . . . and think we can see how things were. We will always exaggerate or downplay events depending on the limited information we have to base things on. So, thinking about how much of an amazing life your partner and his ex must have had together is totally pointless and emotionally exhausting.

Stop! Now is the time to realise that all we are doing by thinking about someone else's past is torturing ourselves. We will never see it exactly how it was, nor would we want to. This is a past before they were dating you. So, judging their behaviour, feelings, or actions is irrelevant as the chances are that had they met you first, they would never have had any of those experiences. And the fact that they are no longer together suggests, firstly, that things probably weren't as great as you are thinking they were or they would still be together and, secondly, they most likely did not and do not want that relationship any longer. Time has passed; they have both changed; your partner has moved on and is now with you. They have chosen to be with you and not with their ex. Regardless of who broke up with whom, the relationship is in the past; it has gone. You are the present and, hopefully, their future.

Even if the relationship worked at some point in the past, it clearly stopped working, which is why they are no longer in it. Just because something worked once does not in any way mean it will work now or at anytime in the future. Your partner will be aware of this. They are most likely not spending their time thinking everything through, analysing every detail, and wishing they were somewhere else. They are with you, in a totally different relationship, and you offer an entirely new set of qualities that must make your partner happy or they would not choose to stay.

One of the most difficult parts in dealing with our partner's past is the thought that he has memories and experiences with other people. When we are in a relationship or in love with someone, we would naturally wish that we were their only love and that no one was important in their lives before us. We find it difficult to think about the person we are with being intimately involved with anyone else. For some, it can even feel like a sort of betrayal, as irrational as this sounds. When we meet someone special, we almost want it to be like a fairytale, being the only person our partner has ever set eyes on and had feelings for. However, in today's world, many people are meeting later in life after a number of relationships, so the chances of being the first person of importance in our partner's life are very slim.

Although their past relationships are a part of them that you cannot change, what you can choose to do is to stop dwelling on them. No good will ever be achieved by torturing yourself about something that is clearly hurtful to think about and will always be an illusion. Our mind and our thought process is not always good to us. It allows us to take a thought and the more attention we pay to it, the bigger the thought will grow. As it grows, it will become more demanding and appear more real until we eventually find it hard to put it at the back of our minds and stop thinking about it.

This will continue until eventually it takes over all of our rational thoughts. Everything gets blown out of proportion and exaggerated until we find it hard to focus on anything other than the ridiculous mess of thoughts that have become all tangled up in our head. So the obvious thing to do here is to start immediately banishing all thoughts to do with anyone related to your partner's past. And if you haven't begun the irrational thinking—don't let a single thought enter your head! Otherwise, before long you will start to believe these thoughts as thoughts end up as emotions, regardless of whether they are true or not. So when these emotions begin to cause physical changes in our body causing us to feel fear and anger, we feel this supports our initial thoughts, so it must be true. We have to distinguish between rational and irrational thoughts to avoid the irrational ones becoming a 'reality' to us by falsely believing them.

There will of course be many couples who are happy to discuss their past with each other and talk about the relationships with their exes. That is not for everyone. For the most part, it really does not do us many favours hearing about this stuff. It is not necessary and does not serve any purpose other than to add fuel to the many fires of jealousy that will burn over time.

I used to think it was fine to ask questions and share experiences. At the beginning of a relationship, people like to suss each other out and get to know one another better. We think our partner's past relationships have had an impact on the person they are today. So we think we want to know more. But do we really? Is it really beneficial to hear any details of things your partner has said or done with other people, especially those they have had feelings for? Surely the only important matters are what is going on in the relationship now.

There are going to be times when we judge our partner by the things that they did before they met us. We may use these things to base our judgement on them, which is often quite unfair. We think that if they had many different partners, or behaved in ways that we would not have done, they are not worthy partners and we can feel angry and betrayed by their behaviour. In these situations, we should appreciate the fact that our partners have changed and those actions were a part of their past. We have all behaved in ways that we are not proud of and whether your partner is proud of their past or not, they are not behaving in this way now and we should think about this rather than focus on the negatives.

It is important to remember that people change, your partner has changed, their ex has changed, and that nothing is the same as it was then. So, focusing our attention on that part of their life really is pointless as it has gone. The past does not exist now and neither does the future. If neither of them exist, why are we worrying about them? The only thing that is existing now is the present moment, so until we decide to start living in it and leaving the past behind us, we can never be truly happy.

When we begin a relationship, we do not generally have the same level of feelings we have when we get further down the line and are involved at a deeper level. Therefore, when we ask questions about the past and receive the response, we think we can deal with it. However, one simple question that you ask can quickly turn into a barrage of questioning which leaves you feeling like you need to know every detail. But this can leave your partner feeling defensive, wary of sharing such details and, more importantly, not wanting to think about and remember all the details themselves! We may obsess, but your partner will most likely prefer not to think about things, putting it at the back of their mind almost like it had never occurred.

When we begin this questioning, we are dragging up a part of their lives that they had moved on from, forgotten about, and hoped that was the way it would stay. They are also very aware, in their rational minds, that all the answers they give out could be brought back up in the future and used against them! Because, although in the beginning we think that this questioning is all part of getting to know them better, before long, the answers that are received play on our minds until we end up having an irrational and deluded opinion of our partner's previous relationship(s) as our mind decides to play on the small detail and turn it into something it is not.

All in all, we end up not only creating a minefield of information for our minds to take totally out of context, but also we are encouraging our partner to talk about a part of his life that in reality, we would much rather he forgot! So, unless we really are one of those people who really has no problem whatsoever with our partner's past, the past is clearly much better left where it belongs so we can enjoy living in the present moment while looking forward to a great future!

Why You Hate His Ex?

You worry that they won't love you as much as they did their ex, care for you the same way, think you are as intelligent, attractive, desirable, etc . . . There are numerous reasons you believe that your hatred of the other person is justified. What you fail to realise is that your partner is not with them any longer, they are with you! Therefore, that other person obviously does not have the set of qualities and attributes that your partner looks for and needs, and that is the reason they are with you—because you do have them!

Any relationship is between two people. Not one (just you) and not three (you, them, and their ex!) So, why is it then that we seem to suffer so much in a relationship by not only thinking we are alone with it all, but thinking that his ex is part of our relationship also, when in reality she is his past and there most likely for a very good reason.

We make the mistake of thinking that we are the ones that are affected when we are having trouble accepting or dealing with any ex-partner of our loved one. However, this is not the case at all as your partner is going to feel the effect full on as they are not only seeing you suffer but also will not be having a fully complete and fulfilled relationship with you because of it.

So, basically, we are creating the very situation we want least. Not only are we causing problems and tensions in the relationship, but by having these feelings we are also keeping their ex very much in the picture when what we really want is for our partner to forget all about them and for neither of you to ever have to think about an ex again.

Obviously, there are going to be many situations where this is just not possible—if they have children together, or work together, or for various other reasons. But what is possible is to create a stress-free relationship between the two of you, which means that when you don't have to deal with the ex, they are not a cause of pain and suffering for the two of you.

There will be various reasons why you feel that you hate his ex. If you are chatting with your female friends, you could probably sit for hours dissecting the woman, finding every single characteristic annoying—shallow, fake, unattractive, and most of all wondering what on earth they could possibly have seen in them in the first place. But mention it to your partner and of course they will just think you are having a bout of jealousy, which maddens you even more! Of course, there are loads of reasons to hate them! They have shared memories with your partner, and no other person should ever have played such a part in their life! OK, the irrational thoughts begin to creep back.

Overall, you are always going to find a reason to be critical. Part of this is because they would probably not be your choice for your partner. It was your partner's choice, at a phase of their life that they have moved on from. Probably from a stage of their life where you didn't even know them. So it would be impossible for you to work out why they were together then, let alone work it out now when time has changed everything. They are most likely very different people from the ones they were when they started out. So wasting time wondering what your partner saw in their ex is quite literally that—wasting time.

It is impossible for other people to work out the reasons that two people are together. Often, we are not even aware ourselves why we were attracted to someone or in relationships with people from our past. The only thing that is easy to work out is that things changed between them, hence they are no longer together. So, just by looking at their ex and basing judgements on the small amount of information you have managed to extract, it is really not possible to work out anything about their relationship. Whatever you do manage to work out, it is more than likely going to be false.

It is always good to remember that no two relationships will ever be the same. The dynamics between two people are unique to them. So just because your partner is all the things you find attractive in a partner, this does not mean they expressed the same qualities in relationships with other people. When you see how romantic or passionate your partner is with you, there is no point thinking this must have been how they were with other people, as everyone extracts different things from a person. It is not possible to be exactly the same with each person you date.

We also hate people from our partner's past as it stirs up emotions within us that we really don't like and definitely don't want to admit that we have . . . jealousy and envy.

It always comes down to fear! Fear of loss, fear of abandonment, and so on.

These feelings are brought on due to insecurity and feeling that you are inadequate. All negative emotions derive from fear and, in this situation, the fear of losing someone (your partner) or the fear that someone else has had or could get something you want. These are very intense emotions and can lead to further destructive behaviour such as anger, anxiety, depression, and resentment.

Envy and jealousy are emotions that have been present throughout many years of evolution. Nerve signals trigger our body to respond within milliseconds of sensing there is danger around. This causes immediate responses such as an increased heartbeat to improve the blood supply, adrenaline increases, and blood pressure and breathing changes, and there is an increased activity within the stomach. All of these responses prepare us for a fight-or-flight response. Our brains are filled with the history of responses from millions of years ago, and we have no control over the sudden and immediate change that is happening.

What we can do next, though, is to become consciously aware of what is happening and the changes that we are beginning to feel. When we are aware, we can then make decisions on how we deal with things, rather than letting natural and often destructive emotions make choices for us.

Jealousy is generally the feeling you get when you have something you want but jealous feelings, connected to what you have, are simmering away. Jealousy can make you feel suspicious and angry. You may be fearful that you could lose something that is important to you.

Envy is more to do with feelings you have when you don't have something, but have jealous feelings towards it and would like to have it if it were possible.

It involves emotions such as a longing and desire to possess something you want but don't have. This can also be something that is impossible to have. For example, you wish you had been in a relationship with your partner instead of that person in the past. This is clearly not possible to change or do anything about, so this emotion can be destructive.

Envy, unlike jealousy, can also be connected to positive emotions as if the desire to have a quality that you see in someone else is put into action so that you work towards self-improvement. It can benefit you so that rather than feeling negatively about something you don't have, you can work towards gaining it.

When envy and jealousy are present together, they can be a toxic combination. By gaining some control over these emotions, we can understand our feelings and rationalise instead of letting anger and rage and other unwanted emotions rise to the surface. We need to learn to control our emotions by taking stock of the situation and asking ourselves how real the threat is.

When we are feeling jealous in our relationship, we try to control it by structuring our lives and that of our partners to try to prevent any situation that may bring on these emotions; however, we actually end up creating the conditions in which jealous feelings occur by creating stress and pressure and constantly having it in the forefront of our mind.

The best way to overcome it is by understanding it exactly for what it is and admitting that you have a problem with it. Recognise how it makes you feel and choose not to go through the negative behaviour patterns that these emotions can bring on. It will not be easy as when you start to feel jealousy creep in, your body has already responded bringing about irrationality, anger, and all the negative ways it feels it has to respond to deal with this.

It is OK to ask your partner for reassurance; however, when they respond, try not to keep asking other similar questions. This will leave you looking and feeling needy and insecure. It is much better to trust in the responses your partner gives and rather than nag for more assurance, try to believe the words that they are telling you. You will hopefully receive the loving response you were seeking, and you can both carry on rather than let the conversation expand into something more.

When you are feeling this way, your entire focus is on your partner, when it should be on you. Turn it around; look inward. What are you feeling? Is it irrational? If so, recognise it. Replace your negative thoughts with positive, loving thoughts. Call an old friend, go for a walk or a jog, read a book. Anything to take your mind off the negative feeling that is taking over you. It will soon pass. The more you do this, the easier it becomes. We just have to train our minds so they will learn not to let negative thoughts take hold of us and we will soon see a huge difference in how much better we are feeling for it and not only that, but how much our relationship has improved also.

When we have problems with low self-esteem, we can also find that we focus more on our partner's exes. People can have low, middle, or high self-esteem. Those whose self-esteem is high feel secure, trust their own judgement, and do not worry excessively about the past or present. Instead, they choose to live firmly in the present moment. People whose self-esteem is low may focus negatively on the past, may not feel good enough for their partner, and can generally feel unattractive and as though their partner will be happier with someone else. If self-esteem is in the middle, you can have periods of high, then periods of low self-esteem, sometimes being rational and at other times insecure and unworthy.

If we recognise that we have an issue with our self-esteem, it may be worth taking the time to work on ways to improve it so that we are less focused with people that make us feel negative and spend more time concentrating on people that are important. Recognise that your partner loves you for the way you are. Do not compare yourself to anyone. You are unique. No one else in the whole world is the same as you. Celebrate your strengths and positive points. You are individual, and if you love yourself deeply, you have a much greater chance of your partner feeling the same way too.

ANGER AND HATRED

A nger is very natural and can be a very healthy emotion. Often, people believe the opposite and so they try to mask anger, believing it to be a weakness, not realising that this will only cause the feeling to simmer inside. This anger will find ways of seeping out, or possibly even being released explosively when least expecting it. Therefore, we need to be able to understand this emotion so we can learn how it feels and ways of controlling it so that it does not control us.

When we are having issues surrounding our partner's ex, we can feel anger in numerous ways. It can be directed at our partner, their ex, at the whole situation, or we can even feel anger towards ourselves. Anger is an instinctive feeling, and if we feel that a part of our life or someone close to us is in threat in some way, we can go into the very basic fight-or-flight mode which prepares us physically and emotionally for action. This can bring on feelings of aggression causing our heartbeat to race, our breathing to get faster, and our muscles to tense and we start to feel adrenaline surging into our body. We are now prepared to act on our initial fears that caused the reactions going on in our mind and body.

This is where we need to take control over how we are feeling and not let our feelings take control of us. It can be difficult to stop the initial responses when we feel some kind of threat, but when we recognise the changes within us, we need to become aware of how we are feeling so that we can effectively control them. We can learn the necessary skills required so that we can manage our reactions positively rather than allowing them to be destructive to both ourselves and our relationships.

When we express anger in a controlled way, we can act assertively to confront the situation so that we can resolve any conflict and work out ways of avoiding it in the future. Before the confrontation, we need to first work out whether it is a real or imagined threat or fear that we are feeling. Although our emotions make us aware of possible danger and produce responses, it does not mean that these responses are based on true events. Take some time to calm the body and mind so you can see things clearly and think things through with a rational mind.

If it is someone else's behaviour that is causing you to respond in this way, then communicate constructively so that you let the person know that their behaviour is unacceptable and that you are not willing to allow it to impact you any longer. If it is the actions of a third party that are causing you distress, again, we must find a way to either confront or make changes so that the consequences of the behaviour do not inflict pain on you. While we can look for solutions to problems surrounding our partner's ex, or other people around us, it is not always possible to resolve them. If this is the case, it can be extremely frustrating and we need to look for ways to cope with the problem in our own way so that it does not lead to feelings of anger and frustration in the future.

We can suppress anger temporarily until we work out ways to express it; however, we need to ensure that we do find a release for it. To avoid anger being turned inwards and causing ourself pain and damage, we need to find ways to let it go without losing control of it.

The first thing we need to realise is that anger is a choice and it can be controlled. While it is important to recognise and act on the emotion, it is vital that we know how to manage it so that it does not become destructive for ourselves or others that are around us. When in a relationship, we can very quickly destroy the love and trust a person has for us through outbursts and explosions that happen when we allow anger to take control of our thoughts and actions.

We are responsible for our own emotions, and we cannot blame others for 'making' us feel a certain way. If we are angry and behave destructively, that is our choice. We have control over how we react to things. Our partners will trigger us to feel certain emotions and sometimes they will do this innocently, sometimes deliberately. What we need to do is to be aware of what the triggers are that cause us to react in this way so that when they do happen, we can be prepared to deal with them responsibly and not erratically.

One thing to make sure of is that you do not repress the anger as this will lie dormant in the mind and body until one day out of nowhere it will unleash itself when least expected. Controlling anger and repressing anger are two entirely different things. It is important that when we feel angry about something, we express it in a constructive way so that we can acknowledge how we feel and release it. We can get to know the changes that occur within our body and mind when we begin to feel angry and as soon as we feel these symptoms coming on, we can immediately become aware of them and develop ways to deal with them. Look at the reasons why we are feeling this way. Use the emotion of anger to look deeper at what is happening. Emotions are ways of making us aware of things, so use them to understand ourselves, others, and everything around us so that we see things with greater clarity and make any changes that are needed.

We can look carefully at the reasons that we become angry so we can trace back to see what triggered these emotions. Often, we will find that we believe we have been treated unfairly or unjustly and this is what has activated our responses. If we pause to look at the whole situation and also the other person's point of view, it will help us see the things from a different perspective and hopefully will help us to adjust our response so that we react in a calm and composed manner.

If anger from either yourself or your partner is out of control and there is no improvement, there are many external sources that are equipped to help. Look for books, courses, or online information to gain help and assistance as once you have learned how to direct and control anger, it will have an immediate and significant impact on your relationship and also your general health.

Sometimes we feel so much anger towards our partner's ex that we do not want to let go of feeling this way. The anger can be accompanied by deep feelings of hatred for this person and the circumstances surrounding them. What we fail to realise is that by holding on to these emotions, it is doing more harm to ourselves than it is to anyone else. It will also have a negative effect on our relationship.

While we are harbouring feelings of hatred, we will never be able to find inner peace and calm. We will be full of tension, anxiety, and destructive feelings, which, even though they are aimed in the direction of someone else, will be doing the most harm to our own emotional and physical well-being.

'Holding on to anger is like grasping a hot coal with the intent of throwing it at someone else; you are the one who gets burned.'

The Buddha

Our feelings of hatred cause us to experience a physical change which causes our fists to clench and our bodies to tense, and we have a wave of emotion sweeping over us that makes us feel like destroying our enemy. Our minds are irrational and full of anger and venom which can make us want to lash out either verbally or physically. These emotions bring out the worst in us and are most certainly not appealing or attractive. We allow negativity to overcome us and our minds fill up with unpleasant and harmful thoughts towards the other person.

Hate is the opposite of love. When we love someone, we generally want the best for them. Our thoughts, intentions, and actions towards them are positive, and we would never wish anything bad for them. Hatred is totally different. We have angry and destructive thoughts and we consume ourselves with resentment, negative thoughts, and harmful intentions for the other person.

To disperse these emotions, we should not only look at ways of calming ourselves temporarily, but we also need to find a way to put an end to the feelings of anger and hatred. Otherwise, they will only resume on a regular basis until we have dealt with the issues surrounding the emotions. We need to also look at the root cause for the emotions and dissect the reasons that we are feeling this way so we can figure out ways to relieve ourselves of these feelings on a permanent basis.

We need to take some time to think things through so we can see what is triggering our emotional responses and why we are reacting in this way. When we look deeper at the cause of our anger and hatred, we may find that a lot of what we are feeling is caused by exaggerated or irrational fears and anxieties. It may be that our fears are justified and there is a real threat which is causing us to respond in this way. Whether it is valid or not, we need to ensure we are in the right state of mind to be able to deal with it appropriately. When we take a moment to breathe deeply and calm down so that we are in control of how we are feeling, we can see things much clearer. We see things so very differently when we are in control than when we are full of rage and fury.

To try to get an insight into the deep-rooted reasons that we are feeling hatred and allowing this emotion to cause us pain and suffering, we should learn to listen to ourselves by taking some time out alone. Lie down or sit quietly for a small period of time, letting our breathing and muscles relax as if in a mini meditation. Look at the situation with a calm and rational mind and explore the different emotions that come to the surface when you think about the person involved. Think through the reasons that you resent and hate this person and then look much deeper at the causes for your negative feelings towards them.

When you look at a situation in this way, without direct input from anyone else causing further complications and distress, you can gently explore on your own the reasons behind the distress you are experiencing. Slowly dissect and uncover all relevant matters that cause you discomfort and unease. Look at the emotional responses that are released and compare them to how you feel when your partner or his ex are involved, and notice how differently you feel when you are relaxed than when you are in direct conflict with them. Do not hold on to any negative emotions that you discover; instead, let all the thoughts and feelings come and go without attaching any emotions to them.

When you feel ready, it can be helpful to write down what you have discovered, and if you feel necessary you can discuss them with the relevant person. Only by understanding why you feel such negative emotions towards someone can you work out ways of resolving the problems. Look at how the negative emotions that you are holding on to are affecting how you feel. Is there any real need or reason to be feeling this way? How much better will you feel when you are not wasting precious time and energy with thoughts of someone that realistically have no place of importance in your life.

We also need to accept that we do not have to let other people's behaviours impact how we feel. We are not in control of how another person acts and we have to accept that we need to find, resolve, and understand within ourselves and not think that we are capable of changing how another person is going to behave. Yes, it is possible that you can discuss issues and people will make changes so that you can resolve it; however, this is not always the case. Sometimes we just need to accept that the changes must be made within ourselves and often, when we do this, we find that other people's behaviours also change because the dynamic is altered.

One of the quickest and easiest ways to resolve feelings of hatred is by having compassion and understanding for the other person. When we take some time to see why another person is behaving in a particular way, we can develop empathy by seeing things from their perspective. Often, people act in a destructive manner because they are hurt or in fear of something, so by looking at things closer from another angle, we can uncover a great deal about the other person. By doing this, we can learn not to take things personally and find ways to turn things around so that we do not think and act negatively, but instead we radiate compassion and forgiveness towards the other person.

The other person may still act in ways that infuriate you; however, there will be less emotionally charged responses as you discover ways to calm yourself, understand others better, and think and radiate positivity instead of being drawn into the negative. You will feel like a weight is lifted off your shoulders when you remove feelings of hatred and anger towards this person. The more you practise it, the easier it becomes until soon they will be no more than just a passing thought without having a painful or distressing connection attached to it.

NEGATIVE EMOTIONS

Thoughts create emotions, emotions create behaviour, and when these thoughts are negative ones, the type of behaviour that is created can only be negative.

Our brain responds to our thoughts by releasing hormones and chemicals which then lead us to experience emotions both positive and negative. When we start to feel negative emotions such as fear and anxiety, we go into an aroused state of mind within which our feelings and emotions intensify rapidly. When we experience a negative emotion, we are prevented from seeing things rationally.

What we need to understand is that we get into a habit of thinking and creating the same thoughts and emotions. We need to stop doing this and think for a moment so that we have a chance to choose an alternative reaction. We can't always control the thoughts that pop into our head, but what we can do is take a minute to recognise the thought and choose the type of rational reaction we take to it. It's a little like the following quote. Often, we are too busy doing things the same way we have always done them, to stop for a minute and think about it and change it if it makes sense to.

'Here is Edward Bear, coming downstairs now, bump, bump, bump, on the back of his head, behind Christopher Robin. It is, as far as he knows, the only way of coming downstairs, but sometimes he feels that there really is another way, if only he could stop bumping for a moment and think of it. And then he feels that perhaps there isn't.'

—A.A. Milne, Winnie-the-Pooh

If we imagine how we were feeling when a negative emotion took form in our mind, we very quickly reach the stage where our actions come into place and we react in ways that seem out of control or based on the high emotion that we were feeling at that time. When we have calmed down, we often see things through a different light as our rational emotions and thinking have come into play helping us to have a more knowledgeable and informed perception of the situation. As it is clear to see the difference in our state of mind, it becomes obvious to us that we should take a moment to try to stay calm and think clearly before we react. If we still can't think clearly after a moment or two, leave the situation and come back to it when you are feeling calmer. You will probably notice that your response is slightly different and this will help to avoid unnecessary conflict.

We copy and repeat emotions and actions that we have learned throughout our lives. It is possible if we have had a parent or person close to us that has behaved in negative ways that we then subliminally take on their emotions as those of our own without even realising we are doing it.

There is a great quote that sums up the fact that we can focus too much on the pain and discomfort within. 'People have a hard time letting go of their suffering. Out of a fear of the unknown, they prefer suffering that is familiar.'—Thich Nhat Hanh. We must be very aware that we can become used to pain and suffering and learn how we can break the patterns so we can become familiar with love and happiness instead.

There can be a range of emotions when it comes to exes, which range from mild annoyance and paranoia to total hatred. One thing is for sure. The more you focus on and allow the hatred to exist, the more it will develop into something that will become uncontrollable. The less time and energy you give it, the less likely it will cause you any pain or trauma. It is important to be aware of these thoughts as they sneak up and when they do, firmly put them back where they belong, in the back of your mind. The more you do this and the quicker you can deal with these thoughts, the easier it will be to be free of them on a permanent basis. The important thing to remember is that you can have total control over your thoughts, and although it may seem impossible to stop irrational thoughts entering your head, you are the only one who can get rid of them.

People hate exes for a variety of reasons, but usually the main one is quite simply this. She was there before you. This can lead to all kinds of feelings such as jealousy, rage, anger, frustration, betrayal, distrust, disappointment, fear, anxiety, envy, disgust, uncertainty, and many more. Any of these emotions is going to have a direct effect on your well-being and relationships with others, especially your partner.

Our emotions have taken millions of years to establish themselves through evolution. They emotions are a big part of what help us survive, so we have to ensure that we have them balanced or they are going to have a massive impact on our relationships, especially with our partner. Negative emotions will also directly affect our health. Emotional responses are proven to have physical effects on the body, and the more negative feelings we have, the more damage we are doing to ourselves on the inside.

Negative energy grows. You have to become aware of negative behaviour patterns or thoughts before you can begin to do something about it. Imagine negative energy as a garden full of weeds. As a weed begins to grow, you must deal with it immediately, from the root. If you do not, it will only grow back and before long the garden will be full of weeds. If we try not to go over and over events in our mind, it is much easier to let go of the thought rather than making the thought and the emotion attached to it grow.

When you notice a negative thought come into your head, do not pay any attention to it. Just take a moment, breathe deeply, and let it go again. The more thought you give it, the more real it will become. It is important at this stage to try and let the thought go away as quickly as it came. At first, this will take quite a bit of effort. It will not come easily. Our mind likes to play tricks with us and will keep putting the thought back into our minds. The firmer we are in dealing with this, the quicker we will gain control of what we think about.

If you find that a thought is persistent and will not easily go, it could be because it needs to be dealt with first. We must spend a little time understanding ourselves and our relationship better so we can work out which of these thoughts are petty and irrational and do not need to be addressed and which are deeper issues which need to be talked about and worked through so that we can find a way of letting go and moving on so that we are not plagued by things that have no benefit or place in our life.

Negative emotions and thought processes can be overwhelming and can literally leave us with no energy, and we can suffer in every aspect of our life. Ignoring emotions that are important and need to be dealt with is not going to resolve anything. The key is to work out which emotions are irrational and unimportant and which are those that need to be dealt with before they become a habit that will be very difficult to break.

We have the capacity to cause ourselves a lot of pain and upsets and the more we behave in this way, the higher level of trauma we create. This trauma eats away at us inside and develops into aches and pains that impact our body greatly. If we broke a bone in our body, we would not just leave it to heal badly and worsen, so why do this with a mental problem that is causing distress? Negative thoughts are like muscles. The more you exercise them, the bigger they will get. The only thing to do is to work out ways to deal with it effectively as it will not just go away by itself.

The scientific term for thought processes is cognition and these processes are such thing as attention, perception, memory, problem solving, understanding, and using language and decision making.

Feeling a certain way can leave us feeling more negative than usual. Not getting enough sleep, hunger, thirst, being too hot or too cold, and basically anything that is off balance with any of our senses can have a direct impact on how we feel that day and can cause us to be more irritable or irrational than we normally would be. Whenever we are going through a stressful phase, it is important that we still eat, drink, and rest enough to ensure that we are in the best frame of mind possible for dealing with any negative feelings we may be experiencing.

Also, regularly exercising has been proven to lower our stress levels, decrease negative emotions such as anxiety and fear, and increase positive emotions such as feeling happier, calmer, and having more energy. This, in turn, will make us less likely to be thinking negatively. Once we are thinking negatively, it is much more difficult to have the motivation to do any exercise. So when we are feeling like this, we must recognise it and, instead of giving in, push ourselves to do something physical, even if it is just a short walk out with nature. We will instantly feel the benefits of this and it should have a reversed effect on our emotions.

When we exercise, we are releasing chemicals called endorphins which lower our perception of pain. It also has the opposite effect as when these chemicals are released, we can achieve a natural high which relieves us from symptoms of stress. As the body temperature increases, this naturally soothes the body, encourages less uncontrolled muscle activity (which causes us to feel stressed), and relaxes the body and the mind. Overall, however little we exercise, it is guaranteed to have a positive effect on us, reducing the negative thoughts and effects from those thoughts and emotions that build up.

PARANOIA AND JEALOUSY

P aranoia is an emotion that can easily creep up on us when we are having issues with exes of our partners. When someone is paranoid, it means they are unnecessarily suspicious about something that they have no reason to doubt and constantly worry and fear that bad things will happen. The more we think in this way, the more our fears feel real as our mind has repeated over and over the negative thought until it eventually feels like it is realistic and will end up happening. Before you know it, you are hardly spending any quality time together and you spend more time thinking about negative scenarios than you do enjoying your relationship.

Quite often, paranoia can seem as though it has come from nowhere. When you meet someone for the very first time, you do not have the same deep emotions that you do as when you get further into a relationship and more deeply involved. It is as your emotions grow deeper and the fear of losing what you have grows stronger that you begin to feel anxious, worry, and doubt everything and all of the thoughts you have turn into insecurities. This can cause you to feel jealous, which then leads to paranoia, and the further the relationship progresses the more difficult it will be to control.

You can be in a seemingly stable and loving relationship where there has been no sign of mistrusting behaviour from your partner, and neither have they ever given you any reason to doubt them. Out of nowhere a thought can enter your head that derives from a fear that you may lose what you have or that there is a chance of it being taken away by someone.

Often, we want to think we own our partner, as though they belong to us as they have committed to being in a relationship with us. We try to control them by determining where they can and cannot go and who they are allowed to communicate or spend time with. This leads to possessive feelings towards them, which leaves us fearful when they take part in anything that we have not had some control over.

Doubts start to enter your head as to whether that person is being entirely truthful and honest with you. You may start to dig for information or any sign that will confirm your suspicion. Anything that you find to warrant your behaviour impounds massively on your already fearful mind; however, any evidence that is found to dispute this seems to get ignored and put to the side as if you are in favour of the incriminating evidence. We don't want to be proven wrong and so convince ourselves with scraps of evidence that there must be truth in what we are thinking.

Everything and everyone that you come into contact with will analyse for any hidden information or facts that could further strengthen the debate that is going on in your head. You almost become desperate to find something that will prove that what you believe is your 'gut feeling' or intuition is not wrong. However, often it is not our gut feeling that is giving us this information. It is irrational thoughts that develop, leading us to believe, with no proof or cause for concern, that our partner cannot be trusted and we feel perfectly justified in continuing this destructive behaviour!

Paranoia can turn you into an emotional wreck and has further negative effects on your self-esteem. It can leave you searching through drawers, pockets, emails, checking call histories, and spying on the other person. There is no limit to the levels that someone will go to when paranoia takes a hold.

> 'Jealousy is simply and clearly the fear that you do not have value. Jealousy scans for evidence to prove the point—that others will be preferred and rewarded more than you. There is only one alternative—self-value. If you cannot love yourself, you will not believe that you are loved. You will always think it's a mistake or luck. Take your eyes off others and turn the scanner within. Find the seeds of your jealousy, clear the old voices and experiences. Put all the energy into building your personal and emotional security. Then you will be the one others envy, and you can remember the pain and reach out to them.'

—This quote by Jennifer James says it perfectly.

Many people have described jealousy as the most painful and destructive emotion they have felt. It literally eats away at you inside and instead of getting better over time, if left untreated, gets worse until it can take over your every waking thought.

When a bout of jealousy strikes, try and listen to what it is trying to tell you about the situation or about yourself. Is it warranted and a warning signal that there is something wrong? Are you feeling insecure about something? Fearful that you may lose someone or there is a risk that you are going to be hurt and need to be aware so you can minimise the risk? There can be various reasons for feeling jealous, and it is very important to take a moment to understand yourself better and work out why you are experiencing this emotion before acting on it.

You may notice that the feeling of jealousy has been triggered through a strong feeling of attachment to someone and when that person interacts with someone attractive or someone they are interested in, you worry that they will be taken away from you. Or it could be that you feel that you are in a position where you are feeling humiliated or embarrassed by the actions of your partner and this builds up inside as feelings of betrayal and jealousy. It may be that there is no real reason or threat for jealous emotions to be stirred, and when you rationalise with yourself and understand this, with practice, you can quickly and easily ease these thoughts and replace them with secure, loving ones to calm your body and mind and quickly recover from the negative effects of this emotion so that you can continue as before instead of letting the emotion take hold. The more you do this, the easier it will become.

Jealousy and paranoia quite literally build walls. In Ireland there is a wall named 'The Jealous Wall' which was built by the first Earl of Belvedere, Robert Rochfort, as he suspected his brother was romantically interested in his wife, so he built the wall to block the view to his brother's house. It brought great distress to the Rochfort family, and he imprisoned his wife aged twenty for the most part of her life in the house; she was only released after his death.

Something as simple as a name mentioned innocently or a chance meeting with an ex-partner or a wrong number on a phone can be enough to instil the deepest fears and jealousies leading us to feel paranoia that our partner is cheating or wants to! This can lead your partner to hide things that there is no need to hide for fear of stirring up unnecessary and unwanted feelings and arguments or telling small lies to cover innocent things up but which they believe will lead you to think they are guilty. This, then, has a detrimental effect on you and the relationship as you believe that if they told a lie there must be something more to it that they wanted to hide.

It can get to the stage where a simple outing to the shops can cause a paranoid person to go into a rage because the other person simply shared a small joke with the checkout assistant or going on a night out leads you to believe that your partner has been eyeing up other potential partners all evening! Before long, it comes to the point where neither of you wants to leave the house together for fear of what will follow due to the numerous things that can trigger these responses.

The only option to save yourself from this and get your relationship back on track is to face the problem full on and wholly commit yourself to dealing with it fully as it is possible to get to the bottom of the issues causing it and become aware of the problem, work through it, and develop a loving and trusting relationship that you can both enjoy without all the negativity and pain that these kinds of feelings can cause. When we do not confront jealousy and admit that we are feeling this emotion, we actually feed it as it is allowed to run wild and free in our mind, thinking up all kinds of crazy scenarios and making us believe there is a real threat. When we accept it for what it is and consciously replace the negative thought with a positive and rational thought, we can begin to change the way our mind deals with the thought and the way it involves our emotions and bodily responses to the perceived threat.

We can become paranoid when we feel that we are not worthy of our partner's love and affection. We fear that they will leave us for someone better than us, and as soon as we see any signs that this could be true or we see anyone that could be a threat, especially an ex-partner, suspicious thoughts begin to enter our minds to alert us to the fact that they may leave us for someone we irrationally think to be more suitable. We need to immediately become aware of the thoughts we are having and take control over them before they develop into negative emotions which will ultimately lead us to destroy our relationship if we don't find ways to work through them.

There are different levels of paranoia. In milder cases, the person may be aware that their thoughts and feelings could be irrational, and in extreme cases people can become delusional, struggling to work out fantasy from reality.

A small amount of jealousy is perfectly normal when under control. It is very common for people to feel a hint of jealousy when they see their partner laughing and joking or embracing someone else. These are our emotions alerting us to the fact that there could possibly be danger following. Our body prepares itself by releasing chemicals and hormones that cause us to behave and act in a certain way. When we are in control of our emotions, we become aware of the way we are feeling and rationalise with ourselves telling ourselves that we trust our partner and know that they would never do anything to jeopardise this trust. When we are not in control, we allow our emotions to take control and one tiny thought develops into emotions that we soon find are raging out of control as our imagination starts to involve itself and before long we are acting irrationally, throwing around accusations, and saying hurtful things which can lead directly to aggression and even violence in some cases. When exercised regularly, jealousy becomes an emotion that grows stronger each time it is allowed to flow freely. It is essential to gain control over emotion to prevent it from being allowed to take over and destroy relationships, friendships, and also your self-esteem.

You need to first of all rationally establish the type of relationship you truly believe you are in. Do you feel that your partner is 100 per cent committed to you and would never do anything to risk breaking this bond and the trust? Do you feel that if there was a problem in the relationship and your partner was unhappy that they would come to you to speak to you about it first before doing anything outside the relationship? Or do you feel that your beliefs and judgements about them are completely justified and your partner is capable of all the things you are imagining and it is just a matter of time before you find the proof?

People become jealous and paranoid for a variety of reasons. One of these may be that you imagine and invent scenarios based on what you think has happened or will happen. In the majority of these cases, your beliefs will be totally unfounded, irrational, and untrue. We cannot ever totally know what has happened in the past with other people and we certainly can't predict the future.

When experiencing feelings of jealousy, many people feel ashamed of this as though they cannot admit to anyone what they are going through and so bury their feelings in the sand and try to carry on as normal. What we need to remember is that everyone at some point in their life has experience of this emotion and when we are true to ourself and confront our feelings, we can take steps at working out what is causing the feeling, whether it is real or fake, and the best way of overcoming it so that it does not grow out of control or lie dormant waiting to explode at any time.

As soon as you become aware of how you are feeling, you instantly have gained some control over it; however small that control may be, it is a start. Just try it! The next time you are feeling any negative emotion, become aware of how it is making you feel and, instantly, you will notice a difference. If you can catch the emotion early on and rationalise with yourself as to whether it is real or fake, you stand a much better chance of dealing with it rationally regardless of how serious the situation may be.

Jealousy can be the most confusing of emotions as often you can totally trust that your partner will never cheat on you; however, the mere glimpse of him chatting with another woman can make your blood feel like it is boiling and your body flush with anger and rage.

Often, these situations progressively get worse due to poor communication and honesty levels between you and your partner. The most important thing to do is to communicate effectively. When you have an irrational fear or worry, gently discuss it with your partner without making him feel as though he has done something wrong. That way, hopefully, he will be open and honest with you and this should put your mind at rest that your fears are based on nothing more than your imagination running a little wild.

People can often function perfectly well in all other areas of their lives and still develop symptoms of paranoia which they can really struggle to deal with. In fact, many people who suffer with it are often very creative and imaginative people; however, it seems in many cases that this imagination serves to create the delusion and paranoia to make it feel real. If someone is suffering from paranoia, it is important that they do not blame themselves entirely as paranoia is a mixture of many things brought together to make a situation seem a genuine fear.

A team of researchers at the Institute of Psychiatry at King's College London interviewed 1,200 people as to whether they thought other people would do them harm and they found that the levels of paranoia were higher than expected. Their findings concluded that 40 per cent of people worry that people are making negative comments about them, while 27 per cent worry that someone is deliberately trying to irritate them.

Researcher Dr Daniel Freeman said: 'We were astonished at how common paranoia and suspicion are amongst the population.

'Understandably there are certain instances when it is important to practice caution, such as taking money from a cash machine without alerting too much attention and walking down a poorly-lit street at night.

' . . . However, our research demonstrates that there can be a tendency to exaggerate our fears.

'Our study shows just how many of us are worrying—probably unnecessarily—about something that might not happen instead of getting on with the more enjoyable and productive parts of our lives.

'We also found in our study that these suspicious thoughts can cause real distress.'

Dr Freeman added that in the past it was thought that paranoid thinking was assumed to occur only in people with severe mental illness as people generally avoided talking about paranoid thoughts. Now that there are effective ways to combat paranoia such as cognitive behaviour therapy and self-help options, people are much more likely to address the issues.

A senior lecturer in clinical psychology at the University of East London, Dr David Harper, agreed that it is possible that paranoid thoughts were probably more common than people realised.

He said: 'People need to realise that these sorts of thoughts are not that rare, and should not be too frightened by them.'

'There are surveys to show that people are much less willing to trust others than they once were,' he said.

He also suggested that it was possible that contemporary Western society and the media played on people's fears by creating a climate of suspicion. If your paranoia is surrounding the actions or thoughts of your partner, it is essential that you work through these thoughts so you can try to resolve the issues surrounding them.

Often when people have low self-esteem, they can become convinced that they do not deserve the good things that are happening or feel that eventually the relationship will fail. Instead of waiting to see what will happen naturally, they sabotage the relationship by creating problems within it. The fear of losing the relationship becomes so bad that they find it difficult to cope with, and in the process they end up destroying the relationship before it has a chance to end on its own. This can be especially true if relationships in the past have come to an end. They believe that this one also will end. However, if they looked at it from an alternate angle, they will see that those relationships ended as they had not met the person they were supposed to spend their life with and now that they are in this relationship, they should appreciate it for what it is instead of being fearful and let the relationship take its natural course.

In the beginning, it is not always possible to differentiate paranoia from real fear. It is important that we fully understand ourself and our fears and anxieties and address any issues within so that we can work out what is real and what is not. If we do not address the issues, we can end up becoming controlling and obsessive, feeling like we need to be aware of every movement our partner takes and being aware of their every movement so that we can avoid any betrayal or future disappointment taking place.

If you are totally happy with yourself and live life in a loving and positive way, you can be sure that the relationship ended quite simply because you did not suit the other person and not because of irrational insecurities and jealousies.

There may be situations where the paranoia you are feeling may have some truth within it. In this case, you really need to look at the facts and details presented, and trust your knowledge and intuition and make decisions based on rational judgement rather than fear and insecurity.

We need to learn to retrain the way our brains are thinking. When a negative thought comes along, recognise it, notice how it feels just for a moment, and then let it go. If the thought comes back again, ask yourself if it is justified. Use your knowledge and intuition to make a rational decision. Try and stay calm; do not let your emotions get involved at this stage and work out if the threat is real or false. If it is false, quickly replace the thought with a more positive and loving thought, and repeat it over and over in your head until you feel calmer and can let it go. Keep yourself busy; do something to take your mind off it. The more we do this, the more we are going to have control over our emotions and actions. If the thought is rational and needs to be acted upon, do not do this when you are feeling emotional. Try and do whatever you can to calm yourself down and then decide the best course of action for yourself.

Jealousy, when detected and dealt with effectively, can actually cause us to have a greater understanding of ourselves and of our partners. It can alert us to the fact that we have emotions that can run very deeply and cause us to act out of character and in a way that when we are feeling rational, we can't imagine ourselves behaving in such a way. As we work our way through our emotions and learn to deal with the negative feelings and reactions that jealousy causes, we find we have an inner strength to control our reactions that we were not previously aware about. Talking through our fears and insecurities with our partner can actually bring us closer together as we work at resolving the problems and creating a stronger, deeper, and more supportive relationship together.

If you find that you have tried all of the above and are not noticing any improvement, or you feel your situation is more serious, then it may be time to look at getting assistance in the form of therapy or counselling. Hopefully, with time and practice, you will be able to work through the issues surrounding jealousy and paranoia, but sometimes external help is required to beat the issue.

If you have ever heard of 'The Law of Attraction', you will understand that quite often, when we focus so hard on something, it can end up materialising. So, the more we think about feeling jealous or the harder we concentrate on situations where these emotions may come into play, the more likely we are to attract these into our life. So, if instead of focusing on terrible thoughts and actions, we think of happy, loving ones instead, we are much more likely to attract these to us and be free from the negative ones.

A loving relationship is one of the most important things we can have in life, so it goes without saying that it is worth doing whatever it takes to get things right. If you have found a loving and supportive partner that is willing to help you with this, then they are worth their weight in gold, and remember that the bonds you create through working through problems rather than ignoring them will only make you stronger!

Just remember that to gain positive results, it is essential that both partners are as open and honest as possible with each other. Both partners need to feel safe and supported for a relationship to fully develop, and committing to resolve problems together will help you build a strong foundation for your future together.

It goes without saying that if the paranoia is leading you to any situation that could be dangerous, you need to get the appropriate help or assistance or make knowledgeable decisions regarding your safety. In this book we are talking purely about relationships and trust issues, so if you or someone else is experiencing paranoia on a more serious note, this needs to be dealt with separately.

COMMUNICATING EFFECTIVELY

One of the main reasons that couples struggle to stay together is due to a lack of honest and open communication. When we talk to each other, it is important that we feel validated and that the other person is listening. It doesn't take long to work out if someone has trailed off and is no longer concentrating on what you are saying; so, for communication to be effective, it is essential that both parties listen intently.

The way we live today with so much technology surrounding us, many people, especially the younger generation, communicate more and more by phone, email, or text. When there are problems surfacing, there is no substitute to sitting down in a comfortable surrounding and being able to talk freely with each other in person about any issues that you would like to resolve. Try not to discuss any important topics over the phone or by text as misunderstandings can occur and it is not always possible to fully get your point across or fully realise your partner's point of view. Whenever possible, wait until you both have the time to talk things through face to face as you will have a much better chance of successfully resolving all issues when you are in each other's presence.

Once you become aware of a problem and begin to look at dealing with it, you have already taken away a great deal of the power it holds. Just by determining the internal thoughts that are toxic, you are already on the way to reducing and ultimately being rid of this type of unwelcome and destructive thinking.

To deal with the thoughts that we feel need to be addressed, it is essential to do this in a way that is going to be as painless and effective as possible. If this means that we need to communicate our thoughts with our partner in order to resolve this, we must do this when we are calm and rational as otherwise it is pretty much guaranteed to result in a huge fight. Nothing will get resolved and the negative thoughts will remain. Only decide to discuss a problem with your partner if you feel that by doing so it will provide some closure as otherwise you are only going to ensure that another argument with no positive outcome will take place.

The first thing to ensure is that your partner is in the right type of mood to resolve this. If there is an issue you would like him to open up about that is connected to his past relationships, it is essential that you are both comfortable and rational as this will help to ensure that the conversation will begin at a place where you feel you are both in an open and honest frame of mind for the maximum result from the discussion.

Think about your typical reactions to things that you don't like to hear about or how you may react if your partner is honest about something that you were not aware about. If you ask your partner for the truth about a situation, you need to be prepared for the response. And if that makes us a little uncomfortable, we need to learn how to deal with it. By reacting badly to the truth by crying, shouting, storming off, or sulking, your partner will be much less likely to want to discuss things fully in the future.

If the information that you are receiving is hurtful or causes concern, then you must voice your feelings regarding this but make sure that you do so in a way that is as calm as possible. This will not always be possible, I understand, but you must remember that the easier you handle the information, the more likely your partner is to communicate in an honest and truthful way with you in the future.

If possible, try not to discuss an issue that you have already been thinking about for some time that day because, as explained earlier, these thoughts can take on an energy of their own and what can begin as a small thing can quickly develop in the mind to something much greater. You will then have emotion attached to this thought and you are not going to be starting the discussion in the same frame of mind as your partner.

As difficult as it is, try to disperse the thought, ride the storm out, and keep your mind busy with other more important issues. A helpful tip is to think of a short mantra in times of need. To do this, you can quite literally think of a few truthful words to put together as a sentence that you can repeat in your head over and over until the irrational thoughts disappear.

Make the mantra short and simple. Here are a few examples:

He loves me; he chooses to be with me.

or

I am his present and his future.

Or you can choose something solely for yourself such as:

I am a unique person who deserves happiness.

or

I will try to only think positive thoughts.

Repeating these types of mantras can be done out loud if you feel comfortable, whispered as thoughts in your head, or you can sit or lie down somewhere quiet for a few minutes and turn it into a mini meditation where you are quiet and relaxed and release any tension from your body and mind and totally let go of anything you may be holding on to.

To do this, find a quiet and isolated spot if possible. Lie or sit down and slowly pay attention to any area of your body that may be feeling achey or stressed. Tense the area and then let go. Repeat this all over until you are feeling totally relaxed and calm. Then gently say the words you have chosen until you are feeling in a better state of mind and then you can let go of the mantra, concentrate on your breathing, and just let your thoughts come and go without holding on to anything or paying attention to anything that comes into your mind. After a few minutes, hopefully you will be feeling free of those negative thoughts and will have replaced them with the positive thoughts brought on by the mantra.

When the emotion from the thought has passed, you can think about how best to approach it with your partner. The important thing to do is to remain as calm, rational, and detached from it all as possible. This will allow your partner to open up and help to resolve the issue. Try to remember that as much as you don't want to be discussing these issues, neither does your partner. He will be very aware that talking about his past relationships is a sure-fire way for war to break out between the two of you. By working through problems in a relationship, you learn to communicate better and in doing so this can create a bond between the two of you that can bring you closer together. Do not be afraid to communicate as effective communication can strengthen a relationship.

Before you begin, remember that staying on the topic of conversation and not jumping from one thing to another is very important to ensuring that the issue you want resolved gets dealt with. Think about what it is you want to say and try to think of ways to say it constructively and without it turning into a barrage of questioning. Remember that creating a safe atmosphere to discuss things at a deeper level will mean that you will have much more chance of resolving the issue rather than just creating more tension and stress within the relationship.

Some basic points to work through when dealing with sensitive topics are as follows:

1. Ask whether it is a good time to talk. It is not a good time to talk when you are tired or stressed, just back from work, on the back of another argument, been drinking alcohol, at work, in the car, on the phone, when guests or children are around. Basically, the best time to talk is when there will be no interruptions and you are both calm and relaxed so you can discuss your feelings without anything else getting in the way.

2. Listen carefully to what your partner is saying and try to remember what has been said. All too often, when we are in a discussion where we are trying to resolve something, we are too busy thinking about what we are going to say next or holding on to one or two words that have been said to truly listen to the other person. By listening carefully and then very briefly thinking about everything before responding will help to keep you calm and also ensure that you have a much more balanced and rational reaction to what has been said.

3. When the other person is speaking, let them get everything off their chest and speak about any points that are bothering them, however

insignificant they may seem. It will be very difficult to remember all the points that have been made, so when they have finished, explain that you have been listening and you want to understand and resolve the issues. So ask them to pinpoint areas of what they have just said that they want to discuss further. This way, they will be able to communicate to you points that they do want to discuss further and let go of any that they just wanted to voice but then let go. Obviously, if there is a point you want to discuss or clarify, you also have the opportunity to do this so you can equally discuss and resolve all aspects so that there are no misunderstandings of feelings left unvalidated.'lkm

4. Try and have empathy with the other person and understand where they are coming from. They will find it a lot easier to communicate if they feel you can see where they are coming from, even if you do not fully agree with what they are saying.

5. Be prepared that the outcome may not be as expected and you may end up verbally attacking each other—denial, blaming each other, tears, tantrums, and walking away from the situation are all things that may occur. Think this through beforehand and how you can try to avoid these things happening.

6. Try not to say anything that is negative. Only use positive words and sentences or it will be guaranteed to turn into a slanging match.

7. Understand the reasons for the talk. Is it so you can clear up a misunderstanding or talk about trust issues? Do you think your partner may have lied or do you want to discuss relationships and friendships that your partner may have with others either now or in the past? Whatever your cause for concern, ensure that you have a clear outline of the reasons for the discussion before you begin and that you make your partner aware of what you want to be talking about.

8. Be realistic. Not all discussions are going to end exactly to suit you. You may have to listen to things you would really rather not hear. If a discussion is to be honest and open, you have to prepare for the fact that it may at times be uncomfortable. Do not fly off the handle if it is not all going your way. Pay attention, listen to what is being said, and try and reach an outcome that is going to be mutually beneficial and, if possible, try and get to the root of the problem so you can both be sure that it will not crop up again in the future.

9. Do not interrupt. This is another way of fuelling the fire as not only can one party not get their point across effectively, but it assumes that what they are saying is not important enough to be fully listened to. Be patient, take turns in speaking and listening intently to one another, and when the person has finished do not extract a few of the words to take them out of context as again, this is most definitely going to create more problems.

10. When you have finished the conversation, ensure that you are both fully aware of the conclusion and that you both feel that you have said all that you wanted to say. It is going to be totally ineffective if one person then goes away feeling that they have not been listened to or understood. And the issue will still be lurking, waiting to return in the future.

11. Try not to manipulate the other person by using emotional blackmail such as crying, tantrums or yelling or screaming.

12. Do not assume that you know what the other person is thinking or saying before they have spoken. We are all individuals with a whole set of our own conditions and judgements, so it is not possible for one person to be able to just 'know' exactly what another person is thinking about.

13. Avoid giving out mixed messages, i.e., two conflicting sides to the same point, or using verbal and non-verbal ways of expressing yourself that are contradicting each other.

14. Don't ask too many questions, especially the questions that don't need to be asked or the ones where you probably do not need to and would not want to hear responses to.

15. Using personal insults or knowledge about the other person. Bringing up sensitive and personal insults is going to be destructive and hurtful. Avoid this entirely as this will lead to further feelings of pain and betrayal.

16. Try not to generalise situations. Saying 'You never . . .' or 'I always . . .' just leads to further disagreements as the other person will most likely argue that they don't or you don't always behave in a particular manner.

17. Quickly recognise when one of you is beginning to feel angry. You may recognise anger as a rush of emotion that comes on suddenly and quickly takes over your mind and body and can make you feel blind rage. At this point, take a moment to compose yourself and calm down, walking away for a few moments if necessary. This way

you can hopefully continue the conversation rationally by stopping the anger before it develops further.

If you feel that the discussion is going badly, see if you can both agree to take some time out. Make a drink, step outside for a few minutes, and just for a few minutes both do something that calms you slightly so you can let go of some of the emotion and tension that has built up and continue to discuss things without both getting upset and frustrated, which can lead to a heated argument.

Learn to compromise as it is not always possible that two people are going to see things exactly the same. Ensure that you see the discussion through even if it takes all night. Walking away, sulking, or keeping unresolved issues inside will just be damaging to the relationship. Remember, above all, that this is your loved one, your soulmate. Treat them with love and respect, and you should see the same affection coming back to you.

It is good to remember that it is not about the amount of conflict that two people have, but rather the way that it is resolved. Problems that are settled with resolution rather than ending with contempt and frustration can help lead to a stronger and more satisfying relationship in the long term. As long as both partners are willing to equally work together, there is no reason why disagreements can't be seen as a positive way of each airing their opinion in a mature and loving manner. By trying to see the other person's perspective rather than just your own, it makes it so much easier to be able to quickly and easily settle disputes before they flare up and out of control.

TRUST

Trust is the foundation for any successful relationship. If trust is missing or if it has been broken, it leads to numerous problems within a relationship and until the trust issues are worked on, it will be almost impossible to have a loving and fulfilling relationship with someone.

Trust gives the impression that we have an unquestionable and total belief in something or someone; however, many of us believe that we trust someone completely, but in reality we may have doubts about different things from time to time. To trust someone is to rely on someone, and this takes a certain amount of faith and courage as if the person does not behave and act in a way that is expected, it can lead to feelings of betrayal, hurt, and disappointment for the person who is trusting.

Often, people who have low self-esteem and low self-worth have difficulty trusting others. They become irrational and paranoid, accusing their partners of things that they have not done. In this situation, the person with low self-esteem can become uncontrollable and over-emotional as their irrational thoughts turn into irrational emotions causing them to behave in ways that are destructive to their partner and relationship. Even though they are aware of how they are acting, anger and rage can take over and it can be very difficult to control their actions. Ironically, by behaving like this, they can ultimately be the cause of the relationship ending, which is something they fear even more than what they are accusing their partner of!

Quite often, when we have trust issues, there is a reason behind it. One of the reasons may be that we have been hurt very badly in the past. This creates a real fear that we may be hurt again and so we subconsciously prepare for this whenever we see any sign of danger approaching. Our minds remember all the details from previous situations where we have been hurt and alert us to it so we do not forget the previous situation and repeat the painful experience. Unfortunately, often we prepare in this way even when there is no real danger; however, we are not consciously aware of it, so we behave in an irrational manner. The key is to recognise when there is a need to worry about our fears and when there isn't. Another reason may be that the person that we are involved with is not truthful or may have behaved in a way in the past that has caused us now to doubt their authenticity. In both cases, we need to work on ourselves so we can be fully aware of the situation and see it with as much clarity as possible to ensure that we react in the appropriate way.

If we have little or no trust in a person, it can lead us on a hunt for further answers. We can become obsessed, looking for any small amount of information to justify the concerns in our head. This can lead us to more revelations as we uncover many other details that are often irrelevant or from the past, and in doing so we end up having even less faith in our partner as we discover things about them that we would be better off not knowing.

If we have been hurt very badly in the past, we can also have trust issues when we begin to feel we are getting too close to someone. This can cause us to try to sabotage the relationship as our mind remembers that in the past we were caused pain by someone who loved us, so when we find ourselves in that situation again, our mind perceives this as danger and causes us to react in a way that damages and sabotages the relationship by preventing us from getting too close. The more conscious and aware we are that this is happening, the better chance we have of avoiding reacting in a way that will destroy the trust and distance us from the other person.

To be able to change aspects of ourself, we must not look only to the conscious mind, but more importantly the subconscious as this is where the majority of information regarding memories, conditioning, and habits are stored. From birth and throughout our lives, other people and ourselves have conditioned our mind. By constantly repeating thoughts, beliefs, and behaviours, we end up seeing things as reality and the truth, when in a lot of cases this is not the case. Therefore, we can reprogramme our minds to change they way we think about things. To do this, we need to fully focus on what it is we want to change and have firm belief in the fact that we can change the way we think about it. Most of what goes on in our mind is self-created as we move into adulthood holding on to thoughts and feelings that have been forced on us as children. As years go by, instead of working hard to change these belief systems and focusing on what we think is true or false, we find it easier to go along with what our mind is telling us must be right.

The same thing happens with trust. We base the fact of whether we trust someone on all the conditioning that we have been experiencing through our lives and make a decision about someone or something based on a past experience without giving this person the chance to prove that they are trustworthy. While it is obvious that we also learn from experience and do not discard everything we have learned and continue to make the same mistake time after time, we must also be very aware that we can use what we have learned in a rational way whilst not holding on to baggage from the past and make a judgement on a person based on what is happening now, not what has happened in the past. It is not fair to cast everyone in the same mould, and therefore we must judge whether we can trust someone in a fair and rational way.

This will be very difficult to do at first, so we must learn ways to break down the forms of conditioning that have taken years to build up. At first, it will be difficult to tune the inside and outside together. On the outside, you want to look and feel happy, carefree, and relaxed, but on the inside you are suffering from fear, anxiety, and scared to trust. While you are learning to recondition your mind, just by smiling and acting happy on the outside, however false it may seem at first, has an automatic response to how we feel on the inside. So, you will immediately feel a benefit as how you are acting on the outside will transmit to how you feel on the inside. To live a happy and fulfilled life, the work needs to be done on the inside so you can get to the bottom of any issues and work through them in a positive manner for long-term benefits.

In any relationship, trust is extremely important. If there are any trust issues, they must be resolved before the relationship can move forward.

To work through issues of trust, the following points can be helpful:

1. Communicating. By talking things through fully, you build trust with each other. It is important to be open and honest so that any trust issues can be broken down and worked through. Listen to

the other person as well as talking to them to ensure that you fully understand each other.

2. Remember that if you never trust the other person, it is impossible for trust to grow. Only by giving trust and seeing that the person has behaved as we expected can we achieve faith that this person will not betray us. If we never trust someone, we are not giving them the chance to prove to us that they are worthy of it. By regularly giving out a little trust and seeing that it was worthwhile to do as as the other person acted as you thought they would, gradually you will feel able to trust more and more until eventually the trust issues will fade and you will have more confidence in your partner.

3. React calmly when you are given the truth. If you react badly when in this situation, your partner will feel that you cannot handle the truth and they will be less willing to discuss things fully in the future.

4. Be reliable. If there are trust issues on either side, one of the best ways to build back confidence is by being able to rely on each other. If either one says something, stick to it wherever possible and try not to let the other partner down. If you both feel safe in the relationship, you are much less likely to have issues concerning trust.

5. Ensure when you are speaking that your tone of voice, facial expressions, and body language all match up when you are talking through issues. Otherwise, it will seem as though you are giving mixed messages or are not fully committed to resolving the issues.

6. Have faith that the other person can handle hearing the truth. Although the truth can be hurtful, it is always better than a lie. By believing this and giving your partner the opportunity to handle whatever is discussed, it will develop trust between the two of you as you communicate and confide in each other.

7. Accept your partner for who they are. You will find it easier to understand that they are human and are going to mess up a little from time to time, not always saying or thinking the same way as you do, while also possibly telling white lies from time to time. Do not judge them so harshly for it and feel that due to this they are not the perfect partner or will be unfaithful or do something to deliberately hurt you.

8. Do not try to manipulate. As soon as your partner is aware that they are being tricked into anything or that their partner is game-playing, it breaks the trust in the relationship and causes communication to

break down. It suggests that the person doing the manipulating thinks they are cleverer or more skilled than the other person and that they can work the situation so they can get what they want and need out of it.

9. Treat each other with love and respect. Regardless of whatever has happened, the two of you are in a relationship together because you love one another and want it to work. Otherwise, you would not be willing to work on the relationship. Therefore, always remember to talk to the other person like you care for them and their feelings and not with an angry, negative tone. The more you speak to one another in a loving way, the easier it is to trust in the other person and feel confident that you have each other's best interests at heart.

10. Be honest. However hard it may be, when you are dealing with trust issues the best way forward is learning to be honest and open with each other so that we know that we can depend on each other to tell the truth when required. Be sensitive to the other person and always consider first what needs to be said and what is just going to be unnecessary and hurtful.

11. Forgive and resolve issues from the past. Whether there are incidents that have occurred in this relationship, or not, understand that if you intend to stay together and work things through together, you need to work at forgiveness and letting go. If either of you have pain or anger that you are holding on to from the past, it will come out in other ways. These wounds become infected and continue to grow until they are dealt with.

By communicating and being honest with one another, you can learn to forgive the past and treat each other with the love and respect that you desperately need to keep a relationship alive and flourishing.

YOU

I n order to love yourself, you first need to learn to accept yourself totally with all your faults and weaknesses. You need to nourish your body and mind to keep it healthy and ready to take on the trials and tribulations that life brings to us.

Often, when we are experiencing difficulties in our relationships, we can question our own emotional and mental health. In order to maintain an intimate and fulfilling relationship and live life to the full, it is essential to have a healthy and balanced mind. Sometimes we can become so stressed out with life that we cannot think straight or make decisions as our mind is full of negativity and our heads feel so frazzled that it seems almost impossible to break free and turn our life around. This makes us feel and act in ways that almost seem crazy as we struggle to cope with how we are feeling inside and also find it difficult to respond in a rational way to other people, especially our partner.

We often take great care of others, our family, our friends. We can even take great care of ourselves on the outside but forget the part of us that needs the most attention and care—the inside.

We are not truly capable of fully caring for anyone else until we learn to treat ourselves properly. Many problems such as low self-esteem, irrationality, jealousy, moodiness, and other issues can arise when we are not looking after ourself properly.

The most important thing to focus your attention on is yourself as if you are not happy and do not love yourself, it really is true when you hear people say that other people around you will struggle too. No one can create happiness for another person. We are all each responsible for our own happiness and for loving ourselves and until we are comfortable with ourselves, we are going to find it very difficult to have a deep and loving relationship. You need to understand what you want from life and from your relationships. We do not always choose relationships or friendships with people that are good for us, and therefore we must be aware of our needs and requirements so that we can make decisions based on what we know and believe is the right thing for us.

People can spend years getting by without really knowing very much about themselves or what they ultimately want. It is always beneficial to take some time out and get to know yourself a little. Rediscover lost interests, hobbies, or friendships. Take time out on your own where possible to do something that feels nourishing.

By looking after ourselves, we can prepare ourselves better emotionally to deal with situations that we may find stressful. Even when we don't have any control of things that are happening around us, we can control how we treat ourselves.

Here are some of the ways we can look after ourselves better so we can be fully equipped to deal with life's more difficult situations.

Never compare yourself to others and at the same time, try not to judge others as when you do this, you are automatically making a comparison with yourself. When you compare yourself with another person or compare what you have compared to what others have, you become vain and bitter as you want to match up or be better and you will only keep looking for something until you find it, which will end up making yourself feel worse. Or you will do the opposite and compare yourself so the other person looks worse, and again you will just end up filled with negativity, which again will just make you feel worse.

We compare our strengths to another's weaknesses, or our weaknesses to their strengths. It is not often that we compare like for like and even if we did, no two people are alike so you will never see the truth in the situation.

So, the only option is—stop comparing! There really is no need. The only reason we compare is to try to make ourselves feel better and it ends up having the opposite effect! We all have positive and negative traits and are unique individuals. Comparing yourself to your partner's exes is a self-destructive pattern. By focusing on other people, you lose sight of yourself. You cannot be living and enjoying your own life fully if you are so focused on someone else's life.

Think more about what it is you want from life, make positive steps to change the things you feel you want to and accept the things you can't change. And while it is OK to look to others for inspiration for positive ways to change your life, do not make the mistake of thinking anyone else is better or worse as each journey is individual to that person and comparing and analysing theirs against your own will just lead you to feel worse. If you see someone looking great on the beach, don't feel negatively towards them. Work out ways that you can eat better and exercise more to feel better about yourself. If you compare yourself to someone who has a better job, retrain, study more, and work out ways of being more successful yourself. Turn the negative feelings straight into positive ones before they have a chance to develop.

One of the things that has a direct effect on our well-being and the way we think is sleep. Most adults should average around eight hours of sleep to be able to function effectively, although some can survive on as little as six hours and others need around ten. As we get older, we still need the same amount of hours' sleep; however, it becomes more difficult to sleep for one complete period for that amount of time.

Sleep has a direct effect on many different areas, and one of them is the brain and nervous system. This then can take effect in the form of emotional disorders, and therefore if we are going through periods of stress, we need to ensure that we are in the best frame of mind to deal with this by resting properly.

Researchers at the University of California,-Berkeley and Harvard Medical School. that has been carried out links the amount of sleep we have to irrational and emotional behavioural patterns using brain imaging.

Twenty-six people aged eighteen to thirty were divided into two groups. One group slept normally and the other group was sleep-deprived and awake for thirty-five hours. Although both groups showed signs of high response at times, the group that was sleep-deprived had much stronger responses due to the prefrontal area of the brain that normally sends out inhibiting signals and was not able to keep the emotions in check.

Although the group that Walker studied did not have psychiatric conditions, the sleep-deprived group showed emotional reactions that were similar to those that had psychiatric conditions, whereas the group that had the desired amount of sleep did not display such strong responses.

'It's almost as though, without sleep, the brain had reverted back to more primitive patterns of activity, in that it was unable to put emotional experiences into context and produce controlled, appropriate responses,' Walker explains. 'They seemed to swing like a pendulum between the broad spectrum of emotions,' Walker said. 'They would go from being remarkably upset at one time to where they found the same thing funny. They were almost giddy—punch drunk.'

'You can see it in the reaction of a military combatant soldier dealing with a civilian, a tired mother to a meddlesome toddler, the medical resident to a pushy patient. It's these everyday scenarios that tell us people don't get enough sleep.'

'Emotionally, you're not on a level playing field . . . Sleep appears to restore our emotional brain circuits, and in doing so prepares us for the next day's challenges and social interactions,' Walker added.

Overall, sleep deprivation impairs judgement, affects the memory, and causes irritability. With all of these side effects, it doesn't take long to work out that this can have a direct effect on our relationships, especially if there is already tension within a relationship. By ensuring that we gain enough sleep, we can be fresh and ready to face the day and rationally deal with any obstacles that may arise along the way.

Think positively. When we are going through a difficult patch, we find it more difficult than normal to think positively. Many people even wonder if there is any truth in positive thinking. The fact that our thoughts change the structure and function of our brains is called neuroplasticity and there have been ongoing studies for many years into the effects of this. Basically, the outcome is that whatever the mind looks for or expects, it will find and create.

When we overreact, the thoughts that are in our head send out negative emotions and chemicals are released into the bloodstream, which then has a direct effect on how our mind and body feel. Our adrenal glands release endorphins that affect our breathing, blood pressure, and heart rate and prepare us for the fight-or-flight mode. The more we focus on these thoughts, the worse we are going to feel. If we do not consciously become aware that we are lingering in this state, these stress hormones end up killing cells in the area of our brain that are essential for learning and our memory. We need to learn to recognise when we are in danger or when we are overreacting to a situation so that we can relax ourselves and come out of this state of mind so our body and mind can return to normal and we can focus fully on the situation in a rational manner.

We need to replace negative thoughts with positive ones, which will immediately have a direct impact on the way we are feeling. You can try it immediately. Think positive thoughts in your head now and you will see how your mind and body instantly feel different. The longer you keep that going, the better the impact will be, not only on you, but others around you will pick up on your energy and will also respond positively as they will also enjoy and benefit from the positive vibes that you will be emitting.

Exercise is one of the fastest ways that you can instantly change the way your body and mind feel. The trouble is, when you are not feeling great, often the last thing you feel like doing is getting up and taking part in exercise. A lot of people exercise to mainly improve the body shape or to lose weight; however, exercise is a very important tool in keeping the mind healthy and balanced and free from stress. It increases hormones that are released when stressed, such as cortisol, and increases endorphins to give you a natural 'high'. The physical release of energy also plays a great part in reducing feelings of anger, frustration, and other negative emotions to leave the mind more calm and balanced.

Many forms of exercise, particularly repetitive, have a similar effect to meditating. As you focus on your breathing and your mind and move your body, you calm and relax the mind freeing it from stresses and tensions, while also giving the body a great workout.

If you do not feel like doing anything strenuous, a short walk out with nature somewhere or even just stepping outside for fresh air can be all it needs sometimes as the air outside is full of negative ions (which are actually positive for you!), which are free from pollution and have a good amount of oxygen in it to uplift your mood and energy level.

Pamper yourself. Everyone reacts differently to difficult phases. Some people neglect themselves, whilst others pamper themselves. The first thing it will do is it will begin to take your mind off whatever is worrying you, and secondly, you will feel great afterwards. Pampering can quite literally be doing anything that you really enjoy doing. For once, indulge yourself and do whatever feels good. Whether it is curling up on the sofa watching your favourite movie, painting your toe and fingernails, running a hot bath with candles and relaxing music, snuggling in bed with your favourite book, or booking an appointment for a beauty treatment, there are various things you can do to make yourself feel a little better. It is only a little time out, but the results will last much longer and you will see the benefit instantly as your mind is clearer and you begin to feel a little better about everything.

Raise your self esteem. Low self-esteem can be a major factor which determines the decisions we make and how we live our life. When we feel negative and think terrible thoughts about ourselves, we end up believing these thoughts and they prevent us from achieving things in life as we believe we are not worthy, or that if we do get good things, we will surely lose them. Having low self-esteem becomes a vicious circle as we believe we do not deserve good things, so we do not attract them or if we do, we find it difficult to keep them. This has a huge impact on our relationships and prevents us from committing to another person for fear that they will leave us for someone prettier, cleverer, funnier, or for some other reason. We need to reverse this thought pattern and have faith in ourselves and our partners that we are a unique individual who is worthy of love and affection from our partner and instantly our lives will improve as we treat our partner better and see how they treat us differently too. We will cover self-esteem more fully later in the book.

Focusing on yourself. Often, you will hear people say, stop focusing on yourself so much or it is wrong to constantly look inwards. It is something that many people struggle with. Should you focus on yourself, or on others more? Basically, it is essential that we do not become overcritical of ourselves, focusing totally on the negative aspects. But, what is meant here is that you should focus on yourself by looking at ways you can improve areas of your life in a positive way, look for the good points you have, highlight them, and use them to change parts of your life that you are not happy with. So, instead of focusing on the bad parts, focus on the good parts. If you focus on liking yourself, instead of getting other people to like you, you will find that before long, not only will you stop caring and judging yourself so harshly about what other people think, those people will probably actually like you more for having such a positive attitude.

While focusing on yourself is a great thing, we also have to be very aware of becoming too insular and not seeing and feeling other people's emotions or situations. As long as we have a good balance and take care of ourselves and know that our needs have been met, we can be in a position to focus outwards and branch out making solid foundations for loving friendships and relationships.

It's a little like when we are told to fix our own oxygen mask first, we cannot help others until we have first helped ourselves.

Be forgiving of yourself. Don't hold on to any mistakes or bad judgements you have made along the way. Use them as experience and something to learn from, but let go of any associated bad feelings or energy that you use to make yourself feel bad. Be compassionate to yourself and instead of getting angry with yourself, accept yourself and don't have such high expectations that are difficult to live up to. Remember that nobody is perfect. We are all unique individuals and everybody, regardless of however perfect they may seem, has their own set of weaknesses. We all make mistakes and when we do, we have to try not to focus on them, other than to learn from them and move onwards and upwards using courage and determination; otherwise, we will allow fear to control us and keep us in the past reliving failures and parts of our life we need to move on from.

Accept yourself and all your strengths and weaknesses. Be honest with yourself, and think about what you are good and bad at, especially within your relationship. Learn to take responsibility for your words and actions and take criticism as a way to improve yourself rather than as a negative comment. Appreciate your strengths and concentrate on improving what you are good at and look at ways of working on the areas that are your weaker points.

When we are emotionally mature, we will benefit from deeper and more successful relationships by not taking situations personally and learning to be secure within ourselves so that we do not let others suffer from any negative emotions we may be feeling.

When we are emotionally immature, we do not take responsibility for our feelings or actions. We blame others for 'making' us feel the way we do and turn the anger or frustration we feel inside on to them to make them suffer. Instead of understanding and having empathy as to why the other person has acted in such a way, we take the behaviour personally and develop negative emotions in response. We then use these negative emotions back at the person by displaying behaviour such as insults, moods, tantrums, tears, yelling, etc. Until we learn to view things from the other person's perspective and constructively deal with our emotions, we are not able to grow emotionally and will continue this pattern of destructive behaviour.

The reason that we fail to grow emotionally is because we are held back by fear. It debilitates us and prevents us from feeling safe to fully explore our emotions as we do not want to take a risk and get hurt. We will stay in this state until we find the courage to deal with this and reverse these actions. As we learn to face our fears, take risks, and see that we survive these risks, we gain further confidence within ourselves, which will help us to grow further and eventually become emotionally mature, enabling us to have more successful relationships.

Being emotionally mature means to accept responsibility for the way we feel and having control over it, to be able to understand and empathise with other, making decisions using a rational and balanced mind, and resolving and forgiving situations with others, to list just a few. Overall, we need to learn not to play the victim, understanding that it isn't always about 'me' and being able to control our responses rather than reacting badly to things that another person says or does or situations that do not go as we would like them to. By taking a moment to consider the situation rationally, we can recognise how we may respond badly to something and instead gain some control so that we do not have an impulsive reaction and instead have a more considered and mature response to things.

Learning to use our intuition is vital. The trouble here is that often we have so many conflicting views and opinions in our heads that we struggle to define what we can trust and what we can't. Intuition is a mixture of working out what is real, memories and data that have been stored and an observation of the situation. When all this is put together, it provides us with the ability to have a gut feeling, a true understanding at a level that is subconscious, and if we tap in to this we can use this information wisely to look inside ourselves and have a sense and true perception which we can base decisions on and make informed judgements with regard to our lives and the constant decisions that need to be made throughout our day-to-day life. By working with our intuition, we can be sure that we are making the correct decisions for ourselves as we are the only ones that know how we feel inside and what is truly good for us.

Some of the ways we can learn more about ourselves and live a totally happy, loving, and fulfilled life are:

Eat well.

Have a good night's sleep.

Exercise regularly.

Read a book, pamper yourself, take a walk with nature.

Stop criticising yourself.

Be grateful for who you are and appreciate yourself.

Connect with others, talk more with friends and family or meet for lunch or coffee, etc.

Think of a positive mantra and keep it close to you; repeat whenever you feel you need to.

Stop thinking terrible thoughts; replace them with loving positive ones.

Watch a good movie curled up on the sofa.

Run a hot bubble bath with candles/ music and relax.

Have a clear-out; if you don't wear it, use it, or if it doesn't look pretty, get rid of it! Take things to a charity shop. You will feel less cluttered, plus feel good by donating things.

Listen to music you love.

Go to the movies. It may feel a little strange, but also liberating to watch your own choice of movie by yourself!

Take a drive to the coast if possible, walk along the seafront, listen to the waves, and let the wind take your cares away.

Invigorate your mind or body. Choose a new hobby or class and do your best to stick to it.

Do something different. Book tickets for the theatre, a football match, a bungee jump, anything as long as it is something you would never normally do!

Cook yourself your favourite meal from scratch. Or bake some cookies!

Slow down a little; meditate for a few minutes or go to a Yoga class or just be still and silent; lie somewhere and slow everything down for a short while.

Study something you are interested in.

Until you feel better, fake it a little. Research proves that as soon as you start to smile, your mood is lifted. So smile, laugh; it really is therapeutic.

Play a game. Find out an old board game you used to love and invite a few people to play.

Enjoy and appreciate every moment. Stop living in the past or the future. Enjoy now.

YOUR PARTNER

At the beginning of a relationship, we can get so caught up in the romance that we fail to see that our partner has any faults or weaknesses. We could have viewed something in the beginning as a quality that we were attracted to; however, when the first flushes of love die out, that same quality then becomes an annoyance.

We have to remember one important factor here: they are not you! They are a unique individual, with their own sets of thoughts, conditioning, emotions, traits, etc. They will not process their thoughts in exactly the same way as you, and they definitely will not act exactly the same. The sooner we fully understand this, the better chance we have of having a stable relationship. We have to accept the other person for their own qualities and individualism and not have such high expectations that are impossible to live up to.

'In an argument, the test of wisdom is the ability to summarise the other person's view before starting one's own.' Haim Ginott.

When we start to have empathy and begin to understand another person, we can then begin to learn effective ways of communicating with them without it resulting in a conflict.

Henry Ford said, 'If there is any one secret of success, it lies in the ability to get the other person's point of view and see things from that person's angle as well as from your own'.

Often, people are misled to believe that logic should make us all think the same way. Not only do our minds think about different things, they also think in a different way to others. This is not limited to different generations, sexes, cultures, or other groups. Even two people that are brought up in the same household at the same time with seemingly the same rules and guidance will also think differently about things.

What we need to gain is a better understanding of the other person. If we can accept each other and that we are different and will not think and feel exactly the same, we are better equipped to have a longer lasting and less stressful relationship.

We evaluate each other based on our own judgements and expectations and in doing so we forget that the other person has different qualities and strengths and therefore are disappointed when they react in a different way than we would. We often find it difficult to control our own responses, so however hard we try, it is going to be impossible to constantly control the responses of another person.

As we have become conditioned throughout life due to all the subliminal messages our subconscious has been picking up since birth, we make judgements and choices and react in a variety of ways based on all the information that we have stored. We need to understand that our partner is an entirely different person with a totally different set of beliefs and conditioning and therefore, even if they agree with us on something, there is a good chance that their emotional responses and thoughts on a subject will vary from ours.

When we fully understand this, we can prevent placing our partner on a pedestal only to feel hurt, disappointed, or betrayed each time their opinions or ideas do not match those of our own. This will help us communicate with each other better and resolve any conflicts of interest before they get progressively worse.

YOU AND THEM

I t is a natural desire to want to be in a relationship and to love and be loved unconditionally. When it is right, it can be the most amazing feeling in the world. People will search high and low and go through many failed relationships looking for that special something. If two people are lucky enough to find the person they feel they have been searching for, expectations and disappointments are bound to creep in as after a short while reality sets in and the dizzy feeling of those first few months fade and the true personalities begin to show through.

There are many different ways to describe love. Passionate love, security love, romantic love, unconditional love, friendship love, modern love, and the list goes on! Every partnership has its own dynamics that are unique to them and falls into one or more of these types of love. Some couples move from one phase to another at different stages of their relationship.

The type of love that many people crave is the unconditional kind. We want someone to love and respect and appreciate every piece of us! We want to feel that no matter what we put our partner through, they will always love us and never want to leave. We are often very unrealistic with desiring this kind of love. The main reason for this is that we often don't have unconditional love for ourself. We judge ourselves over every tiny mistake, making ourselves feel terrible for anything that goes wrong and we regularly don't even like ourselves, let alone love.

So, in asking someone to love us unconditionally, it is clear to see, in order for them to be able to give us what we desire, we have to learn how it feels to love ourselves in this way, so we can fully appreciate and wallow in that feeling when it happens from an external angle. And importantly, we can then learn to love unconditionally in return.

We need to be prepared that loving unconditionally can sometimes be painful as it may be that the unconditional love is not returned. You have to remember that you are choosing to love without conditions and restrictions, and therefore you are not loving to get something in return. You are simply loving. And importantly, we can then learn to love unconditionally in return.

When you recognise the type of love you have in your relationship, you can look at aspects of what it offers you and whether it is the type of love that you desire and need to be fulfilled in the relationship. If you feel that something is missing or that you are not happy with an aspect of it, it is important to discuss this with your partner as with a little work and joint commitment any relationship can make positive changes so that you are both receiving all the things you want from it.

Social anthropologists describe romantic relationships as being similar to a contract. We love someone, and therefore we expect to be loved back and not only loved; we have a huge tick list of all the requirements we need and want from them. When this other person does not deliver all these things and falls slightly off the pedestal we have placed them on, we feel let down and betrayed as if they can't possibly love us if they are not as perfect as we were hoping they would be! And all of this, quite honestly, is setting the relationship up for failure from the start.

When we are in a relationship with someone who challenges us, it is often because there are parts of ourselves that we struggle with and have issues with. There are parts within us all that we can change; no one is perfect. Often, we place ourselves in relationships with a partner who highlights our negative traits and makes us take notice of the parts of our personality that we need to work on and change.

When we are in this kind of relationship, it is easy to begin to feel resentment towards the person who makes us aware of our weaknesses. We should, however, be grateful to the person and see that they have come into our lives to help us work through our issues and be grateful that they have helped us to confront parts of ourself that when dealt with thoroughly will result in our being a happier and move loving partner.

When we fail to see these difficulties as lessons that we need to learn from, we can feel angry and bitter towards our past and feel like we are unlucky to constantly meet people that are not good for us. We will continue repeating over and again these same lessons until we become aware that they are coming back and will continue to come back until we focus on the root cause and deal with it.

If we seem to constantly be in dysfunctional and destructive relationships, it is very important to recognise that we are attracting and attracted to these kinds of relationships entirely so we can repeat over and again the same lessons until we are ready to challenge ourselves and make changes within. We can become deeply attracted to people who we know bring out our weaknesses and arouse our deepest insecurities, fears, and painful experiences from the past. We need to accept that these types of relationships will leave us with emotional scars that need to be focused on and healed to avoid developing a negative pattern that will continue to be destructive and damaging for us.

By listening to ourself and really feeling and experiencing the emotions within ourselves, we can learn a lot about how much pain and fear we are feeling inside and think back to what may have happened in our past to have made us now feel this way, or what belief system we have set up inside our minds that is causing us to think and feel a certain way. By breaking down each part of our thoughts and emotions, we can understand more about ourselves and why we feel the way we do. Until we truly understand what has brought us to feel this way, and show love, compassion, understanding, and forgiveness to ourselves, it will be almost impossible to move on from it and fully love and care for another person.

Sometimes it is difficult to deal with these issues by ourselves as there can be a great amount of emotion attached to past experiences. If this is the case, then we should consider discussing it further with either a partner or friend, or if you would prefer a counsellor or professional person whom you do not know and have no connection to may also be an option for you.

It doesn't take long for two people who connect with each other to start to feel emotional attachments. When two people bond together, they can go through what seems like an emotional roller coaster as they progress in the relationship and deeper feelings form.

Attachments in relationships take many forms and come from spending prolonged and repeated time with a person. You can even form attachments with a person you do not particularly like just by having repeated contact with them. This is also the reason that some people struggle to end a relationship, even if it is not going well or they are no longer in love with that person.

If the attachments are very strong, they can bring bouts of anxiety and fear into the relationship as the worry that the person will leave or the relationship will somehow come to an end will cause negative thoughts and emotions to take place. If this happens, it is important to recognise and deal with the root of the cause and work through these issues so that you do not become too dependent or reliant on the other person as this can be suffocating within the relationship.

We often believe that we are only happy or sad because of the actions of our partner. We rely on them and allow them to be in control of our emotions rather than taking responsibility for our own feelings. As soon as we realise that this other person is simply just triggering these emotions and we are capable of experiencing any of these feelings on our own through our own actions and choices, we can begin to step towards a more balanced and stable existence.

Unstable and fearful thoughts can happen when we do not recognise that we are in control of our own levels of happiness and worry that if this person is no longer with us, we will not have these same experiences when we are on our own. This can lead to feelings of panic and a desire to control the other person and we end up behaving in a possessive way to prevent any chance that this person will go, taking with them all the ways of triggering our more positive emotions.

The sooner we realise that we are all capable of living our lives in a state of happiness with or without another person to trigger these emotions, the happier our relationship with ourselves and then with others around us will become. We need to take responsibility for our own emotions and live life in a way that makes us happy and stable, and then we can build relationships with others based on a strong foundation and, instead of having dependency on another person for our state of mind, we can choose ourselves whether to react and respond to another person's actions.

Do not be afraid to be your true self in front of each other and show emotion if you are happy or sad. Bottling up emotions will have negative consequences as they will store inside and be released when you least expect it. Laugh out loud when you want to and cry as hard as you need when you are in pain. Do not be afraid of the reactions of the other person as the most important thing is that you are true to yourself and your partner should love and appreciate you, strengths and weaknesses included.

Because people can very quickly form attachments to another person, it is for this reason that people advise slowly getting to know another person before committing to them or spending too much time with them before you become too deeply attached and too involved. That way, if you are not very well suited to each other or you do not feel the partnership would be beneficial, you can walk away from the relationship early on before you have got in too deep and it becomes painful to walk away.

Relationships make or break for numerous different reasons. As two people in a relationship are unique in the world, the way their dynamics are created is individual to only them; therefore, it seems somewhat impossible to give a scientific or blueprint solution as to what will guarantee to work. Also, it is essential to understand ourselves, each other, and the relationship as a whole so that we can work through things together as a couple and reach solutions and compromises that will work for us. No one else can possibly accurately diagnose the relationship between two people. It is very difficult to understand ourselves completely, let alone work out another person or another person's relationship with someone else.

The deeper we look at ourselves and acknowledge and work through issues within, the greater chance we have of being able to coexist in a loving and stable relationship.

When you are in a partnership with someone, it is imperative that you both have clear guidelines of your expectations. When two people are on different wavelengths with regard to basic guidelines of what is and what isn't acceptable, cracks will not take long to surface.

One of the main reasons that couples struggle to stay together is due to a lack of honesty and open communication. When we talk to each other, it is important that we feel validated and that the other person is listening. It doesn't take long to work out if someone has trailed off and is no longer concentrating on what you are saying; so, for communication to be effective, it is essential that both parties listen intently.

The way we live today with so much technology surrounding us, many people, especially the younger generation, communicate more and more by phone, email, or text. When there are problems surfacing, there is no substitute to sitting down in a comfortable surrounding and being able to talk freely with each other in person about any issues that you would like to resolve. Try not to discuss any important topics over the phone or by text as misunderstandings can occur and it is not always possible to fully get your point across or fully realise your partner's point of view. Whenever possible, wait until you both have the time to talk things through face to face as you will have a much better chance of successfully resolving all issues when you are in each other's presence.

Every day, each of us is experiencing and learning new things, and each of these things will have a subconscious effect on our relationship. As we grow and change, our relationship needs to evolve also so that we can try to ensure that both people in the relationship have the same requirements for the present and the future.

If there are problems that arise in the relationship, the only way to completely resolve them and get over them is if both partners work together and are willing to understand the problems and then commit to resolve them.

However hard things get, try not to get into a pattern of threatening things, such as leaving the relationship, telling people intimate secrets, cheating, etc. It is not a healthy road to go down as these threats, although often said in the heat of the moment with no truth to them whatsoever, create trust issues within the relationship as they put a tiny doubt in the person's mind that if they have thought it and said it, there is a possibility they could do it.

Also, continually threatening to leave a relationship and then not doing so has a pointless effect as the other person will just think that you have threatened so many times and not gone through with it so why would this time be any different. Threats are childish and are said when a person feels they are losing control of the situation and become angry. It is best to avoid this type of behaviour at all costs.

We have to remember when choosing to respond to positive and negative patterns that we are not training a puppy dog. We are far more complex than animals and need a lot more understanding and empathy when we have issues and problems to overcome.

Choosing to react to issues in a relationship by ignoring and rewarding good and bad behaviour is not going to have the desired effect we would hope for. Often, people react and respond to another person's behaviour due to the dynamics that go on within that relationship, so we may have to consider that we may need to retrain ourselves slightly before we look at asking others to change.

There will always be a certain amount of moulding and compromising within a relationship, but we must not forget that a lot of a partner's traits will be a part of who they are and probably part of the reason we initially fell in love with them. Their carefree attitude and boundless energy may have started out as attributes, but we now find them irritating and annoying. These types of things are essential to their personality and feeling free to be who they are. We must realise that we cannot and should not try to change a person. We have to carefully consider the qualities and characteristics we want and need in a partner and whether we are committed enough to make a relationship work if these ingredients are missing. It's your line, and you decide where to draw it.

Another very negative way to behave is by sulking, moodiness, or ignoring your partner if they have done something that has offended, irritated, or hurt you. This just prolongs the situation, leaving it unresolved, and can leave you both feeling angry, frustrated, or upset. It is an immature and childish way to behave and will only have a further negative impact on your relationship. If you do need some time away to calm down, or need to get away for a short while, explain this to your partner fully so that you are both aware of how you are feeling and this can give you both a little time to think about what has happened and respond rationally to one another.

The quicker that any disputes or disagreements can be resolved, the sooner you can get back to being happy together. Communication is always the key to rebuilding the relationship when things go slightly off track.

When going through a difficult patch, it is beneficial to rekindle the friendship within your relationship that often can be lost amid constant bickering, emotional dramas, and fighting. We are sometimes too busy concentrating on the love or the passion or fighting that we forget about the foundations of it all—the friendship! We often forget to see our partner as our friend, someone we can rely on and who is there for us through thick and thin. We should take time to remember how to laugh and have fun with each other. Find something that you can both enjoy together and get away from the constraints of daily life and enjoy just being the two of you. Think back to the early days where you would stay up all night talking or making love without a care in the world. Leave love notes for each other, breakfast in bed. It doesn't have to be anything major; it is often the simple things that we love most. As often as you can do something a little crazy together, make some memories!

Talk freely with each other about your dreams for the future, things you would like to do, places you would like to visit. Making plans and having a similar outlook for your future lives will not only help to ensure that you are both heading along in the same direction, but it will also help you to bond together as you plan ways of working towards achieving these dreams.

Talk about expectations, both yours and theirs. While discussing these expectations, make it clear to each other where your boundaries lie. When setting them, be realistic and do not have such high expectations that make it impossible for a person to live up to.

Another thing that causes major issues within a relationship is thinking you know what the other person is thinking and can read their mind. The fact is, you don't know, will never know, and cannot possibly read another person's thoughts. You either have to trust your partner and believe that they have your best interests at heart, or make a judgement based on rational thought and knowledge as second-guessing what you believe them to be thinking is only going to lead to conflict and misunderstandings.

Watch your partner's body language so you can understand them at a deeper level and recognise signs when they may be feeling uncomfortable, upset, or worried. Don't always wait for the other person to say when something is bothering them as an attentive partner will notice when a mood has changed or when there is something bothering you.

While it is always good to be attentive, don't think that you know what the other person is thinking or that you can read their mind. The fact is, you don't know, will never know, and cannot possibly read another person's thoughts. You either have to trust your partner and believe what they say and that they have your best interests at heart, or make a judgement based on rational thought and knowledge. Second-guessing what you believe them to be thinking is only going to lead to misunderstandings and conflict.

When you are in tune with your own feelings and emotions, you are in a much better position to understand and empathise with someone else. Being able to identify with your own emotions well and those of your partner will help you tackle any issues before they develop deeper. While it is important to look out for signs of distress in your partner, if you ask them if there is a problem and they say everything is fine, do not push the situation. Just let them know that you are there for them if they want to talk; don't try and tell them that you know what they are feeling or second-guess their emotions. We can never know what someone else is feeling, so just trust that they will come to you if and when they decide they want to talk things through.

Although we know we will have a deeper and more fulfilling relationship if we can be open and honest with one another, this can often be a really difficult thing to do. We fear that by showing our true selves with all our hidden faults and weaknesses our partner may not feel the same way, so we conceal parts of ourself and hide our emotions. We fear that they will not accept us fully if they knew every detail, good and bad, so we try to only show our more positive traits and hide sides to us we would rather not deal with.

In the short term, this may be fine and you may get away with this kind of behaviour; however, if you meet someone special with whom you wish to spend a big part of your life and very possibly your whole future, it will be very difficult if not impossible to live life concealing parts of your personality that you do not wish them to see.

The following are tips to put some fun and enjoyment back into the relationship:

1. Date night. Arrange in advance a night that you are going to commit to, just the two of you. Whether it is once a week, fortnight, or

month, set the date and stick to it. Use the time to date each other just as you would have done when you first met.

2. Cook their favourite meal from scratch if possible, light a few candles, and play some of your favourite songs as background music.

3. Choose a sport that you can do together to keep yourself fit and healthy. It doesn't matter if is is only a light sport once every couple of weeks or you go further and join a gym to regularly attend together. Exercising together can be a great bonding experience and will both be a little more inclined to stick to it as you can support and encourage each other when you feel like giving up.

4. Book a getaway together. Whether it is a night, weekend, or longer, just getting away on your own without any distractions can instantly put the spark back into the relationship.

5. Make some time for a proper lie-in together. Spend a lazy Sunday morning with breakfast in bed, newspapers, a movie; just relax together enjoying every moment of it.

And here are tips to keep the relationship healthy and strong.

1. Whenever possible, try to go bed around the same time. This can create a great intimacy and bonding by getting into bed together and snuggling up before relaxing and preparing for sleep. It is a good time to have some quality time without interruption.

2. No game-playing! Obviously, the emotional kind (the fun kind is perfectly acceptable.)

3. Never insult or use name-calling as a way to gain control or power over the other person. It is cruel and childish and will instantly do damage, often long-lasting, to the relationship. Remember, for every 100 positive things we hear, we always seem to remember that one negative and hurtful one! Just don't do it. Ever!

4. Always try to think of the other person's feelings before speaking or acting, especially if it concerns dealing with the past.

5. Don't compare each other to people from the past, i.e., all my ex girlfriends were saints compared to you . . . or my ex-boyfriends all used to go to the gym! These comments are extremely hurtful and will be remembered! Even though they are not said as true reflections and are often just said in spite, they are extremely destructive ways to communicate, so think carefully before speaking, regardless of how angry you are feeling.

THE POWER AND THE BALANCE

T he power struggle within a relationship is something that is visible in almost every partnership at some stage. It goes without saying that all relationships will have some issues with power at some point, even if it goes unnoticed. A small amount of give and take—allowing the other person to make decisions and take the lead from time to time—is perfectly natural and healthy. However, power within relationships can sway out of control causing not just relationship problems, but can leave one person feeling unloved, unworthy, and powerless. Power most certainly does not automatically bring happiness. So if you are the one with or without the power in a relationship, it is vital to address the issues to try to obtain a healthy balance so that both partners can thrive and feel secure and validated.

Often power differences begin when one person feels that they are not worthy of the other person, or feels that they love the other person more than they are loved. It can also be the opposite. One person might think they are a better catch, more attractive, have a better career, could get someone 'better', etc. There are various reasons for imbalances.

What starts off as just a thought or belief in the mind can then cause you to act and behave in a way that will put your relationship off balance as the other person picks up on the vibes that you are giving off and the things you say and do. Soon enough, the one who is perceived to be loved more or loved less or a better or worse catch than the other person can begin to feel that it must be true, and subconsciously a negative dance between the two people begins. By changing our thought pattern, we take away the belief that another person is better than us. Replace the thoughts with positive assuring ones about yourself telling yourself that we are all equal and no one deserves or should ever be treated differently from another, especially if those two people are in a relationship.

To maintain a healthy balance, each individual needs to have self-esteem, confidence in themselves, and to know that they deserve to be treated with love, affection, and care. We have to stop putting others on a pedestal thinking they are more worthy than ourselves. We should get to know ourselves better by thinking through and writing down our limits and boundaries, and when someone crosses them we need to know that we will take a stand and action to ensure that we are not consistently treated in the same way. We must be strong and value ourselves and treat any obstacles as lessons to be learned along the way so we avoid repeating negative cycles which end with us feeling worthless with low self-image and self-esteem.

Although we must allow for a certain amount of shift in power from one person to another, it is important to be aware when the balance is consistently uneven so that you can find out where the problem lies and fix it before it deteriorates further. If both people have the same desire to commit and make the relationship work, it is beneficial to a lasting relationship to speak to each other about our expectations and needs.

When we can clearly outline our ideals and communicate them to our partner, we have the chance to work together to see if we are compatible together and can be happy and fulfilled in the relationship and therefore prevent misunderstandings which can cause pain and frustration. If the other person cannot meet our needs and is not willing to change, we need to decide whether we are then willing to accept this. If we are, then we need to fully compromise and work out ways to manage the relationship. If the other person is not committed to change, we need to realise that we are not capable of changing another person. We will either gain or lose power within the relationship by trying to force someone to give something to us that is not available and this can create a dysfunctional and destructive relationship full of disappointment and conflict.

If a relationship is going well, the struggles are less of an issue, but when the relationship begins to go through difficulties, problems with power arise to the surface and a battle to achieve it begins. If the relationship is an unhealthy one, it can be very clear to see who is holding the power.

It might seem strange but we actually give other people the power and strength to repeatedly behave however they want towards us regardless of how much we may disagree with the behaviour or how much it hurts us. We allow them to do this mainly by not setting out firm guidelines and sticking to them and also by constantly forgiving behaviours that we do not want to tolerate.

When we say to someone that we are going to do something and then we don't do it, we are giving away our power as they will have seen that we do not stick to our word, so they see this as a sign of our weakness. It is essential that we act on our words and that we don't keep sending out mixed messages and empty threats if we hope to have a balanced and healthy relationship.

When there is balance and harmony within a relationship, generally, there is no requirement to focus any attention on power and people are much happier to give and take more.

In a relationship, people can be overfocused on who is right and who is wrong and this can lead us to fight to defend our innocence or prove the other person's guilt. We have been taught all our lives that we should always do the right thing, so we can go to great lengths to maintain this and if someone tries to prove otherwise we can become defiant and stand our ground, which can lead to a struggle to gain power. The same situation occurs if we feel that someone else is in the wrong. We are determined to prove our point and sometimes we can go to extremes to do this.

No one should ever feel weak, helpless, or powerless in a relationship. By feeling these things, we are actually allowing someone else to contribute to and have some control over our emotions. Sometimes we rely on others for our happiness and to make us feel loved and appreciated or as though we are worthwhile to someone. If these feelings are not validated, we can end up feeling hurt and angry with low self-esteem.

We can get into a power struggle as we feel fearful and anxious about being in a relationship where we feel that we don't have much control over our future. When we meet someone special, our lives are generally changed. This can be a small or a huge change depending on the commitment and lifestyles involved. We mistakenly believe that by retaining our share of the power, this will prevent us from getting hurt further down the line as we can 'play games' with the other person. We falsely believe this will protect us from pain and disappointment as we are in 'control' of the situation. In reality, this will only lead to us being more susceptible to getting hurt as we are not being true to our feelings and emotions and are acting and reacting to the other person with the sole purpose of maintaining the power.

When we stop playing games and start to define what we want and what the other person is willing to give, we can avoid being in a relationship with expectations and delusions. If we learn to accept each other and communicate openly and honestly together, we can work through issues and obstacles without always trying to 'score points' and get one up on the other person by trying to prove that we are right and they are wrong.

While boundaries and guidelines in a relationship must be clear, it is also important not to be unrealistic and that we accept that we all have our faults and issues. Communication and negotiation are the keys to working through what is and isn't going to be acceptable. As long as we are not willing to compromise ourselves too far within the relationship, we can bend and sway with the other person to obtain a compatible partnership that isn't based on games and manipulation.

People are often fearful of laying down the law at any stage of a relationship; however, if it is done in a calm, clear, and constructive way, it can set a firm foundation for the right kind of relationship to grow upon. Just be aware that timing is vital when having this conversation as if it is done too early into a relationship, it can seem too demanding and overbearing. All relationships move at different speeds, so there is no set time to discuss this, however, being aware that it is important to weigh up the relationship properly to ensure that both sides are equally ready to communicate to each other what it is they want, need, and are willing to give.

If one person has invested much more time, energy, and emotion into a relationship, they can feel that the other person holds the power and this can leave them feeling vulnerable and weak. It seems that if you care or love much deeper than the other person, you automatically pass them the power to control and manipulate the relationship.

'The power of all relationships lies with whoever cares less.'

Michael Douglas—Ghost of Girlfriends Past.

There are plenty of theories on 'playing' in a relationship to stabilise this unbalance. However, communicating your needs and desires for the relationship and seeing if the other person matches up and is willing to give the same is the only true and honest way of knowing whether you are in a relationship with a good healthy balance so that you are not living in an illusion, never really giving or receiving more than you should.

People also feel that if they open up too much to the other person and let the other person in by sharing personal details of their past or secrets and confidential details, they then have given the power to the other person as they have shown signs of weakness and those details can then be used to hurt and manipulate in return. Then the person who has disclosed and trusted this information can either feel and act like the 'weaker' one and thus gives some power to the other or they can then try tactics to rebalance the power by playing games of manipulation to level things out.

It is for these reasons that it is important to communicate effectively with each other so that you feel secure and confident that the other person is equally committed so that you can be open, honest, and truthful without feeling that you are leaving yourself open to future betrayal or this openness or pain and disappointment.

By communicating and working through issues and difficulties in a relationship, we can offer ourselves the greatest growth both as a couple and as part of a relationship. We can learn about our own and each other's strengths and weaknesses, working together to gently and lovingly support and recognise ways we can grow and face our shadows. If we can do this in an environment that is secure and protected, we can have the capacity to discover and develop our inner self so that we can rid ourselves of past demons that can continue to haunt us throughout our life, sabotaging and destroying relationships along the way. When we learn to deal with and confront these issues, we can stop repeating patterns that will prevent us from true happiness. By doing this, we reach new levels of love, respect, and commitment within the relationship, strengthening bonds and proving that communicating effectively is the most effective way to a long-lasting and fulfilling relationship.

And remember, if you communicate honestly and the other person does not have all the things that you need and desire in a relationship, do not take this personally. The other person is a unique individual with their own set of conditioning and characteristics. While we would like our partner to be able to reach all of the expectations we expect from a loved one, it is not always that simple to change the habits and ways of a lifetime and if this is the case and you cannot be compatible, it is important to accept this and not take it personally and let it affect your self-esteem or blame the other person, feeling bitter and angry that they are not what you want.

It may be that you are aware of the power struggle and you are trying to have a balanced and fair relationship with the other person, but they seem determined to game play and manipulate in a desperate desire for power. If this is the case, it is important to try to communicate with the other person explaining that you don't want to involve in this kind of dynamic. It is then up to you whether you accept that this is how it is going to be until that person decides to change, but it will be hard to be in this kind of relationship without either feeling unfulfilled or ending up game playing yourself to achieve a balance.

Power can be gained and lost within a split second. It can move from one person to the other with a simple word, body language, gesture, or facial expression. It can be gained and lost through how we treat another person. For example, if we receive a text message from someone and take an hour to respond, we can find that they take two hours to reply to us. Then begins the psychological game where we will take six hours to respond and so it will go on until frustration, pain, and anger take over and conflict within the relationship appears. This can often be quite simply that someone has a good reason for taking so long to reply. However, when people within a relationship are desperate to gain some power, they will deliberately not give the benefit of the doubt so they can exert their point. By quite simply having faith or communicating, you can resolve the issue instantly rather than trying to reclaim some power by playing a game.

Game playing has one very basic purpose—to feed insecurities and self-inflated egos. Mind games are mostly played when one or both parties are emotionally immature and are insecure within themselves. They may also be fearful of showing their emotions and feelings and are scared of committing in case they get hurt. Quite often, someone who resorts to playing games has been very badly hurt in the past and many have emotional scars and baggage. This can make someone scared of feeling like they are 'leaving themselves open' to getting hurt again, so they close off and only give a little of themselves at a time believing they can then control the chance of being hurt again in the future.

If you are both authentic, independent, and have self-respect, instead of playing games with one another, you can maintain a good balance without the need to manipulate. Instead of waiting to see the other person's hand before you deal yours, be open and honest and see if that is reciprocated. If it is not given back, understand that it may be due to the other person feeling fearful of being hurt. They may have closed off part of their ability to freely love and be honest and open due to painful situations from their past. When we can show unconditional love and care for another person, it is much easier for the other person to respond to it. If you do not receive the response you need and desire and instead are on the receiving end of psychological games, it is only you that can make the decision as to whether you want to persist and see if the person will open up to you, or if the relationship is not what you are looking for as game playing can leave you feeling unfulfilled and ultimately damage your self-esteem. If one person in the relationship plays games and the other person susses this out, it can be an instant turn-off and they will lose trust and respect instead of joining in with the game. Although it is called 'game playing', it is not usually fun for either partner and a negative dynamic can set in which can be very difficult to break.

Often game playing is nothing more than a habit. From very early childhood, we have been taught a variety of games, some requiring us to be cunning and manipulative to trick the other person so that we will be the winner. We were taught it is not good to lose, so we develop a variety of skills to make us sharper so that we can be 'stronger' than our opponent. This is evident in board games, physical sport, computer games, and even in the classroom and workplace. We are constantly striving to show our strengths and hide our weaknesses to get further in life. Therefore, when we are in a relationship with another person, it feels totally natural to carry all of these skills over so that we can show our partner only our good bits and hopefully shield them from seeing our weaknesses. However, as natural as it feels to get into this dynamic, it is important to realise that this is the one place where we are not trying to 'get one over' on our partner or prove we are better than them. If we are in a relationship with someone special, we should show them love and respect and only want the best for them, see them as an equal and not as an opponent whom we are trying to score points against. It can be very difficult to learn to drop our guard as we feel we need to be careful and wary so that we can protect ourselves from showing ourselves fully and risk getting hurt. But it is only when we can learn to be honest and truthful with ourselves and the other person that we can have any chance of having a relationship that is not deluded and fake and based only upon what we and the other person choose to show. We can never be truly fulfilled if we are only giving and receiving carefully selected parts of each other. Although it can be terrifying to be the first one to open up and speak from the heart, until we do this, we really cannot ever have the kind of relationship and love that we are hoping for. If we show our feelings and the other person is not feeling the same way, it is better to find that out sooner rather than later as trying to trick someone into feeling something for us is never going to be the basis for a long-lasting and trusting partnership. Apart from anything else, why would anyone want to be in a relationship where they are in an illusion of what is really happening and are only there because of manipulation and trickery. This does not mean that you should live as an open book, telling the first person you meet everything there is to know. It is quite simply about not using manipulation and deliberately holding back to achieve reactions and responses from the other person. You can move as slow or fast as you desire in the relationship, but by having authenticity and being genuine with your partner you can avoid prolonged heartache and confusion trying to work out what the other person is thinking and feeling, instead of having the courage to face the situation and stand some chance of working out if they feel the same way too.

Two people who are in a relationship will always come across situations where they both feel they are in the right. It is not often that both will admit to feeling that they are in the wrong, though! When both parties feel they are equally right and have strong arguments as to why this can lead to a deadlock whereby no one wants to back down, frustration, anger, and tension can ensue, leaving both parties failing to see the other person's reasoning.

When this happens, you can become aware of the situation by thinking of things from the other person's perspective instead of your own. Take a moment to see where they are coming from and why they would be feeling this way. As soon as you step into someone else's shoes and view things from a different angle, it can really help you to work through issues by accepting and appreciating that we are all individuals with our own ideas and beliefs that condition our thinking. By doing this, we may find it easier to step down and be the first one to call a truce and accept that from time to time we will just see things differently. There will be no right or wrong, and therefore no argument is required.

As long as you both talk through why you feel the way you do, there should be no need to battle it out in a heated way. By doing this, the balance in the relationship is restored to an equal level as neither has been 'proven' right or wrong. The quarrel can be quickly resolved with both parties feeling validated, understood, and significant.

To gain a healthy balance in the relationship, both partners' emotional and physical needs should be equally met. If there is one person who creates more drama and demands more attention consistently, the other person can be left feeling drained and exhausted and this can end up leaving them feeling unfulfilled within the relationship. It is vital that both emotional and physical needs are addressed and met so that both partners are fully aware of what the other person wants and expects from the relationship.

By having open and honest communication, it will help both partners to find ways of giving and receiving so that one person is not doing all the receiving or vice versa. There will be periods when one person may need more support and be more demanding, and then at other times this will shift to the other person. This is absolutely fine. An unbalance will only occur when one person constantly takes without equally giving anything back. To do this, all you have to do is make time for each other and listen to what your partner needs so you can keep your relationship in balance and be sure you are aware of your partner's needs so you can mutually express love and affection to increase the close bond and intimacy you have with each other. Although we can give and receive to express and show our love, we must also remember we are each responsible for our own basic levels of happiness and should try not to rely on another person to achieve this or have unrealistic expectations that they cannot fulfil.

You can also help to maintain the balance by creating positive notes after negative ones have occurred. If you have had a terrible row or things have been going wrong, replace those emotions and words with positive ones to maintain harmony and show that you love one another.

If the relationship is swaying too far one way and your partner is becoming disinterested, one of the worst things you can do is to cling on desperately to that person, suffocating them with overbearing words and actions. This will seem unattractive and needy and can be a huge turn-off for anyone. It is better to let your partner know how you feel and be honest and open and then give them a little space to think clearly.

From time to time, people can get a little scared or overwhelmed when a relationship moves into different stages, and sometimes one person may need a small amount of space to deal with this and move forward. By still being yourself, loving, and fun to be around, your partner will much quicker to readjust, have a little time, and should then bounce back like there was never a problem. Do not make an issue about it or turn it into a stressful situation and you will stand a much better chance of riding the storm and coming through it together to the other side.

When two people are together and are committed to making the relationship work, you can also help to find the balance in each other. You can notice changes in your partner and help to lift them up when they are down, comfort them when they are upset, or care for them when they are feeling unwell. If the relationship is healthy, two people can work together to look out for each other and constantly restore the balance in the other person whenever it is needed.

When the balance is equal, you will feel in sync with your partner and this will allow for a deeper and more intimate love. It is hard to experience the emotions of true love when you are either extremely hyper or feeling very down. Only when we are in a calm and balanced state can we have the clarity to see things as they are and appreciate the euphoria that comes with total care, love, and respect without power and mind games preventing this.

FRIENDS WITH HIS EX?

Relationships can also suffer incredibly when there is unresolved history with someone from the past. Similarly, if one half of the couple has a friendship or is in contact with an ex and they are continuously fighting or arguing or if there is underlying bad feeling surrounding it, if either you or your partner is still holding on to someone from their past or has hidden or open feelings about an ex-partner, it will be very difficult to fully commit to this relationship.

When you are suffering in your relationship from issues that are linked to a person from your partner's past, it is vital to realise that when you ban or force someone to stop doing something, it can often become more desirable. When we make demands on our partner to end contact with someone, they will possibly feel resentful towards us. Instead of having the desired effect, this may lead them to hide the contact they have with their ex, which creates further mistrust and distance within the relationship. Rather than trying to control the situation, you can work on ways to understand the reasons that you feel this way so you can work on resolving the problems as they will not go away on their own.

You can start by communicating with your partner as to the reasons they are in touch with their ex and decide whether the reasons are acceptable. Often, people stay in touch with an ex-partner because they feel they are familiar to them and can empathise and understand them better, so if they are going through a tough time, it can be so easy to turn to an ex-partner for advice. It may be that they have things in common with their ex and enjoy their company on a platonic level. There may be unresolved feelings which could stem from guilt from the breakdown of the relationship, or it could be that there are still emotions felt for the ex-partner that still have not died down so they have not fully got over the relationship.

There are so many reasons that a partner could be in touch with an ex-partner that it is impossible to list them all as they are unique to the individual. Talking through your feelings with your partner can help to bring to the surface the reasons so you can either work together to find a resolution or realise it is time to make a decision and walk away from the relationship.

Unfortunately, not many relationships end amicably. Usually, one person has decided that it it is time to break up and the other person is the one that ends up with their heart broken. When someone has made the decision to end a relationship, it can be a much gentler let-down if you say you still want to be friends. At the time, this is not such a problem as it is just between the two people. Usually, neither will have moved on at this early stage or have anyone else's feelings to consider. Problems can arise when either party moves on and meets someone new. This can cause problems for any of the individuals involved. The ex may still harbour feelings which can lead to a variety of problems for all involved. Or it could be that the new girlfriend or boyfriend feels threatened or uncomfortable with the friendship continuing. And the other person may struggle to work out a comfortable balance between not hurting their ex's feelings and making sure your new partner is secure and comfortable with the situation.

When you consider a friendship, it is usually with someone you trust and care about and know that they only have your best intentions at heart and vice versa. If there has been mistrust in the relationship and either party lied, cheated, or behaved in a destructive way that caused the end of a relationship, it can be difficult to see why someone would want to stay friends with someone that has treated them this way.

Another consideration is the amount of time that has passed between a relationship and a friendship. It is going to be much easier to have a genuine friendship with someone if both parties have had sufficient time to allow the feelings to fade and come to terms with the relationship being over before moving to the next phase. If only one partner is over the relationship, it can be incredibly painful for the other to be around, especially when a new relationship enters the horizon. When all the emotions have settled down and both are equally ready to move on, then it can be possible for a successful friendship to form.

If either party feels jealous, angry, hurt, betrayed, insecure, guilty, or any other negative emotion whenever they are around the other person, it will not be a healthy friendship. It is better to take time out and heal before beginning any kind of reconciliation that would lead to being back in touch. The same goes if the opposite feelings occur such as desire, lust, longing, or any similar feeling that you would have for someone whilst in a loving, committed relationship.

Quite often, people choose to be friends with an ex to let the relationship go gently. If you have spent a certain amount of time with someone, you can grow comfortable with each other and familiar, and spending time with this person can be a hard habit to break. You will naturally miss the good and bad parts about a person and may want to keep this person in your life to make the parting easier. It may be that you have shared good memories together and while you don't want to be in a relationship with the person, you would still like them to share a small part of your life as a friend.

If the relationship just drifted apart naturally and both parties fell out of love but still care for each other in a platonic way, then a good friendship can form where there is no fear that either party is interested in anything other than happiness and well-being for the other person. They may be perfectly comfortable and accepting of any new relationships that form and hold no jealousy or ill-feeling that can cause problems. When this happens, it can be perfectly normal to try to continue a friendship harbouring no feelings from the past.

For many people, this is not a problem and they can balance ex-partners and new partners perfectly with no feelings of jealousy or betrayal. However, for many others, this triangle will not be acceptable and will carry with it a whole series of issues.

Dealing with your partner's friendship with an ex can be a painful and frustrating experience. Even if you trust your partner completely, it can still make you think and feel irrationally and think crazy thoughts if they spend time together. Your mind can start to play tricks imagining all sorts of scenarios when realistically it should be reasoning that if they wanted to still be in a relationship together, they would be. They broke up for a reason and probably a very good one. They are with you now, not them.

They have moved on, hopefully got over it, so there is no reason whatsoever to feel worried or concerned. In an ideal world! The truth is, regardless of how much we tell ourselves that, it does not make it any easier to accept. For some, the thought of an ex still being in the picture, at any level, is one that you would just really rather not have to deal with.

If the ex is still around for circumstances beyond their control, for example, if they study together, work together, or have children together, it can be difficult as you may not be able to see the light at the end of the tunnel as you know the ex will be in the picture for a very long time, even forever in some circumstances. In these scenarios, people have to try to rationally see that their partner is not 'choosing' to have their ex around. They are there simply due to the situation at that time and it is up to us then if we want to deal with this and accept it or if it is something we will really struggle to cope with.

If you decide that you are willing to stay in the relationship and accept the situation, it is often wise to discuss with your partner exactly how you feel about the friendship or contact they have and see if you can agree on some basic ground rules. Just explain to your partner that by setting boundaries of what is and what isn't acceptable, you are both aware of the type of friendship your partner will be having. It is not about a control thing; it is just so that you can both avoid misunderstandings that may occur in the future if you have not properly discussed how you both feel about things.

Once you have made the decision to accept that your partner has contact or is friends with an ex, it really is better to come to terms with it and not make it a constant point to argue about. Conjuring up romantic images of the two of them is just going to cause you pain and is a waste of time and energy, so needless to say, don't go there! As soon as any kind of thought comes into your mind, distract yourself and replace it with a positive and trusting rational thought. Soon enough, your fears will vanish and you will feel much calmer and more accepting of the situation.

There is no point in saying you are willing to accept the friendship and then quarreling about it or upsetting yourself. This will just make you both unhappy and serves absolutely no purpose other than destroying the relationship you have together. Trust that your partner loves you and respects you and would not do anything to risk this and unless you have any justification to think the opposite, you will both be much happier without filling your life with unnecessary stress and worry that you cannot do anything about.

However, if there is a good reason to have doubts and fears about your partner seeing his ex on a regular basis, it is essential that these fears are dealt with fully. Unless you confront the issues they will not go away, even if you try to brush them away. If you have a genuine concern, thoughts will continue to enter your head until you have discussed and received answers surrounding the doubts. By setting some time aside to talk through your fears, you can share with your partner how you are feeling and hopefully receive an open and honest response to quell any concerns you have. Try to reassure your partner that it is not that you do not trust them, but that you just want to be able to calmly and rationally cope with the friendship, knowing the reality of the situation so that your mind does not fill in the gaps with all kinds of ridiculous scenarios.

If, after the discussion, your concerns and fears are not calmed and you feel that you have good reason to doubt your partner, you have to conclude on your own judgement as to whether you will be able to cope with the friendship in the long term. Allowing your partner to be friends with an ex is not for everyone, so do not feel a failure or totally irrational if you choose that you are not willing to accept this. At the end of the day, it is all about personal choice and it is ultimately your decision as to what you will and won't accept. You know what you can and can't live with, so ensure that you have come to an informed and well-thought-out conclusion before you make any decision. Otherwise, in the future, when you look back with a rational mind, you may see things very differently and have deep regret that you made the wrong decision as you let your emotions cloud your judgement.

If your ex is friends with his ex through choice, again, it can be extremely difficult to deal with. Usually, these friendships are clear when you enter a relationship, so you can discuss with each other what is and what isn't going to be acceptable. It is important to weigh up whether you think you will be able to handle the friendship as if you cannot, it is going to cause huge problems for you all, which will be destructive for your relationship.

Boundaries need to be set if a friendship is going to continue without any doubts or fears arising. Talking about deep emotions and things they used to like about each other can cause feelings to resurface. Spending time together alone in places that can cause suspicion to arise is also not usually a good idea, unless of course each party is 100 per cent confident that there are no concerns surrounding what may happen between them both. Each of them should be able to freely discuss their new relationships without either party feeling upset or jealous. Your partner's priority should now be you, so they should not cancel plans with you if their ex demands their attention; nor should they be running around doing chores they once did whilst in that relationship. To have a good balance, the friendship needs to be one where each party is equally comfortable with the other and neither have any fears that there is any manipulation or hidden agenda.

Weigh up the friendship. Is it just a social networking friendship? Do they meet up, or do they have mutual friends in common so they will socialise together? Do they talk, text, or email regularly? If you assess the level of friendship they have and what it means to you and your relationship, it will help you to explore your feelings surrounding this so you can work out how you feel towards the level of friendship they have. It is easy for others to say that there should be no problem with accepting your partner's ex; however, we are all individuals and have different expectations, and we are free to choose whatever type of relationship will make us the happiest. Just be sure you are not being irrational with your thought process and that you try to work through any issues you may have yourself before you decide to end a potentially wonderful relationship.

If you choose not to accept it, explain thoroughly to your partner how you are feeling and that you cannot be in a relationship with him while he is good friends with this ex. Do not give ultimatums as this will be damaging for your relationship if you decide to stay together. Clearly explain your feelings to your partner and although it seems drastic to end a relationship because of another person who should not be a threat of any kind, it is your decision and only you know what will and won't make you happy.

If your partner decides that they are willing to sacrifice the friendship for the sake of the relationship, be sure to let them know that you are not asking them to do this. You are merely stating your limits and are making a decision based on what is acceptable for you. It is up to your partner to make whatever decision suits them and whatever they decide, that is totally their choice. Making demands and ultimatums will cause bad feelings, so instead of stamping your feet or using manipulation, just clearly think about what you want and what will make you happy and only when you are totally sure that it cannot work, then discuss fully with your partner. That way it gives your partner a chance to understand how you are feeling, so they can work out for themselves whether they are willing to cut the contact with the ex to save the relationship or work things through with you.

If you have concerns that your partner has not got over his ex, or has feelings deeper than friendship, it is vital that you address this and talk things through fully. Often, people get furious with their partner if they speak well of their ex and when they haven't got any bad words to say about them. This can lead you to think they do this as they still have feelings for them, but often it is quite the opposite. While we are holding on to feelings of pain, bitterness, and anger from a previous relationship, we will find it very difficult to stay calm when talking about the person. If there are emotions still attached to an ex, they usually are evident as the words that are spoken about them or about the relationship will be fuelled by mixed emotions.

On the one hand, they still care and possibly love their partner, but on the other they are resentful that things did not work out and the relationship has come to an end. Although this is not always the case as everyone is different, it is worth understanding that if all feelings are quelled and your partner can speak fairly and genuinely about his past relationships, without having the need to put them down, then quite often there is nothing at all to worry about and it is a very good sign that he is over their relationship and has moved on.

Huge problems can occur if your partner's ex still has feelings for them and has not got over the relationship. First of all, before you begin to panic, you must remember that if your partner loves you and you trust him, there really is nothing at all to worry about. You cannot allow any feelings that an ex may have to ruin the relationship that you have now. After all, that is possibly what they want most, so your relationship will fall apart and they can get back together. Try to remember that at this stage, if your partner wanted to be with them, they would be. So trust completely that they are with you through choice and that is where they want to be. The past is history and unless you have any reason to believe otherwise, it is securely done and dusted and your partner has moved on. You cannot hold your partner responsible for someone else's feelings or for the fact that their ex has still not moved on.

Although your partner cannot control someone else's feelings and actions, they can take steps to avoid it affecting your relationship. If their ex is making it very clear that they want to rekindle the relationship or they are struggling to move on, it is important that your partner communicates effectively with them to let them know that the feelings are not mutual. The sooner your partner sets the boundaries with their ex, the easier it will be for them to understand that any attempts for a reconciliation are futile. If they are friends, this may be difficult to do, but it is much better to be clear and honest so that there are no misunderstandings and the ex does not get the wrong message.

Your partner may find it awkward to confront their ex to make it clear that they do not feel the same way, especially if your partner is a genuinely nice person. When people end a relationship and move on, they often feel guilty for the pain they have caused the other person and don't want to do anything to hurt them further. Even if they were not the one who ended the relationship, they may still find it difficult to explain to their ex that they have completely moved on.

Your ex may feel that they owe it to their partner to be there for them in times of need, especially if they feel their ex is emotionally unstable. Even if the ex is causing trouble between you both, due to the history between the two of them, your partner may still find it difficult to tackle the situation. Try to be understanding and patient and appreciate that your partner may be uncomfortable with this.

It is important that the ex has respect for your relationship if they want to be a part of your partner's life, and if they don't it will be almost impossible for you to continue to date each other with this third person creating waves. If they are no longer friends, a simple call or email from your partner to let them know that they have moved on and are happy in this new relationship should be sufficient. If they are still receiving unwanted attention from their ex after your partner has made it clear that they are no longer interested, then you can either decide to contact them yourself explaining that you would like them to leave your partner alone, or in extreme cases it may be that you need to take it further and seek professional help.

If your partner's ex has not moved on and there are children involved, it is not quite so simple. However, clear boundaries need to be set and your partner needs to outline his feelings firmly so that there are no misunderstandings on either side. While your partner will still be there to discuss and deal with matters regarding the children, they have to make it clear that matters outside of this are not their concern. Otherwise, confusion and misunderstandings can occur on all sides and it will also potentially cause serious problems within your relationship.

Once your partner has made his feelings absolutely clear to his ex, then hopefully this should be enough to reduce the contact considerably. Quite often, exes continue to communicate as they feel there is some small hope that the feelings will be reciprocated. If your partner does not actively encourage or respond to any emotional behaviour, then their ex will most likely see that they are wasting their time and energy and begin to move on. If they see even a glimmer of hope, they may continue trying to control and manipulate your partner, so it is important they are not given any mixed messages to encourage behaving in this way.

If your partner is being harassed by phone, email, or texts, although it can cause disruption, it may be an option to block them from being able to do this. Otherwise, in extreme cases, changing their numbers or email addresses can also be a way of stopping this unwanted attention. If there are children involved, they can have another phone that is only for communication when the children are with them and it is only to be used in an emergency. If all else fails and there are no children involved, they can advise that they will seek an injunction if the contact continues.

Overall, friendships and contact with ex-partners are going to be as unique to each relationship. Only you know what you can and can't deal with or what you are willing to put up with. If you are not happy and confident that the friendship is warranted and you feel that it affects your relationship, then you need to decide to do whatever makes you happy.

The friendship will most likely fade over time, so it should hopefully become less of an issue as time goes on. However, if you do not want to accept the friendship, it is vital to make your feelings very clear and once you have covered all other options, it may be time to let the relationship go if it is making you desperately unhappy. We all want to feel that we are a priority in our partner's life and if this is not happening and there is doubt and insecurity due to an ex-partner, it can seriously affect your happiness and self-esteem.

If you do decide that you don't want to deal with this friendship, be sure before you end the relationship as you don't want to have any regrets, especially if all your fears are unfounded and irrational. In time you may look back and realise there really was nothing to be concerned about, so talk it over with your partner fully, calmly, and rationally. Also, remember that nowadays, especially with the amount of technology we have for keeping in touch with each other, it is becoming much more common for people to keep in contact with each other once a relationship has fizzled out. If you end this relationship, there is a good chance your next relationship may also encounter the same issues.

Deal with any insecurities or issues you may have with yourself and your own self-confidence. Only when you really feel there is no other option, then make a decision as you don't want to lose the chance of true happiness with someone very special because of worry and fear over something that is nothing more than basic contact between two people that once dated. If necessary, talk it through with a good friend or even a therapist so you can voice your concerns and really be sure you have made an informed and thought-out decision so you do not make a choice you will one day regret.

IS THE RELATIONSHIP IN TROUBLE?

There are many signs to look for to see if a relationship is in trouble. People regularly overlook these signs and think that all relationships get this way after a while; however, ignoring the signals will only lead to further breakdown and possibly the end of the relationship.

We often do not notice that there is a problem until it is too late to do something about it and then say we had no idea that anything was wrong. It doesn't take much to keep a check on your relationship and if both partners are honest with their feelings, it is very easy to become aware of issues before they develop into major problems. Even if both partners aren't open with one another or if they don't communicate well together, it is still possible to be in tune with what is happening within the relationship by watching out for changes and differences within yourself and with your partner.

We can go through life with an image in our minds of the type of person we want to spend our lives with. When we finally meet someone who matches up to our mental image, we project all our hopes and desires on to them. We desperately want them to live up to our expectations and meet all of our demands. As we progress deeper into the relationship and the first flushes of love wear off, we begin to see the actual person behind the illusion we have created. All of their bad habits and irritating ways slowly become more visible and things that we may have turned a blind eye to in the beginning can become major issues. Fighting and arguing can break out leaving both partners feeling angry and resentful wondering why their ideal person has turned into someone completely different whom they barely recognise.

Before it gets to this stage, it is very important to understand that having unrealistic and high expectations about a person will be sure to lead to frustration and disappointment. Everyone has their own set of faults and weaknesses and will never live up to the demands put upon them when they have been placed high up on a pedestal.

Be realistic and accept each other for who you are. Recognising our own and each other's weak points and working on them together will help to build strength and bonds within the relationship. Understand that we are all human, and we all make mistakes and have our negative traits. Appreciate each other's good points and focus on the positive.

One of the worst things you can do when your relationship is in trouble is to try and sweep the problems under the carpet, hoping they will go away and the relationship will miraculously improve on its own. This is not going to happen. When there are problems, they need to be faced and dealt with or they will lie in wait and explode when you least expect it.

Accepting when there is a problem and taking steps to repair it is the only way to successfully build a solid and stable relationship that can stand the test of time. If you try to avoid issues that come up, over time they will only get worse. Ignoring your partner or the issue, remaining silent or being in a mood to try to deflect from the problem will lead to further tension and destruction. Keeping communication open and allowing each other to speak freely and honestly about any matter that you feel needs airing will help to avoid problems building up and escalating out of control.

If two people are equally committed to making the relationship work, no obstacle is too great to overcome. By working closely together, you can find ways that work best for you as a couple to help get through difficult patches so that you end up feeling much closer and stronger as a couple.

By looking at your relationship together, you can begin to see where the problems lie and how you can resolve them. Take some time out to discuss and write down important points that are bothering each of you or things that you would like to improve. Once you have made the list, either keep it to work on it together or agree to destroy it at the end of the discussion, whichever works better for you both.

When having this kind of heart-to-heart talk, try to ensure that the atmosphere is relaxed and you are both in the right frame of mind for talking things through. Although a little deep, you can begin by looking at your childhoods and if both of you are open to discuss this part of your life, you can write down feelings both negative and positive that have strong memories attached to them. If there were emotions that were not met when you were younger and you felt periods of pain or neglect in any way, talk through with each other if you feel comfortable and note down any points you feel could be areas to work on.

By looking at how each of us felt as a child, it will help us to understand each other at a much deeper level and will help us to empathise and support one another. We can work together to confront issues within ourselves that need to be recognised, accepted, and dealt with. If we feel secure to talk with one another in this way, it can help to develop bonds and strengthen the trust that is vital within a relationship.

We can also look at how we treat each other and our communication weaknesses. When we write down how we have been feeling, it can make it seem even more real, so this can be a good exercise together if we really want to make changes and break negative patterns that have been building. Taking time to get to know and understand each other a little better will assist us in all aspects of our relationship as we can sometimes be too general with how we see each other, whether we have only just got together or been together for years. We often only see the illusion we have built up of the other person instead of the true character that lies behind. The more we learn about one another, the easier it will be for us to communicate with one another and have a successful and long-lasting partnership.

A few areas we can look at are:

1. How often we criticise each other
2. Forgetting to appreciate the thoughtful things we do for each other
3. Putting each other down when alone with each other or in front of others
4. Not showing respect for one another
5. Listening to each other without interrupting
6. Honesty and loyalty to one another
7. Feeling confident to openly and honestly say how you feel
8. Showing affection and passion for one another
9. Spending time alone together
10. Do you fully trust each other?

When a couple fail to act when the relationship is in trouble, it can fall so badly apart that it is difficult to put it back together. We should view our relationship as an active and living thing which constantly needs to be nourished and cared for so that it can evolve and grow at the same rate as the people within it. Otherwise, it will break down and both parties will either separate or stay together in a way that can cause resentment and bitterness, with neither one receiving anything positive from the communion.

We must always accept responsibility for our own happiness and state of mind and not rely on our partner to try to fix how we feel. While a partner's behaviour obviously can directly affect us dramatically, ultimately we are each in control of our own day-to-day state of mind and can choose whether we allow a person's actions to impose on our emotions. This is often easier said than done. However, by living a fulfilled and nourishing life, we can maintain a good balance of strength and happiness that will help us in dealing with life's ups and downs when they arise. We should try not to wallow in negative situations of being dragged down and beaten emotionally as the more often this happens the harder it is to pull ourselves back up.

One sign that is evident that a relationship is suffering is when one or both partners stop telling each other that they love each other or how much they mean to one another. In the early stages of a relationship, we often compliment or take notice of our partners and find time to tell them all the things we are attracted to. As time goes on, we can become complacent and take each other for granted and feel that they already know how we feel, so there is no need to constantly say it. Therefore, it is vital to a loving relationship to reinforce these things on a regular basis to remind and show your partner how much they mean to you. However, it is true that actions speak louder than words, so it is important to follow this up with treating each other properly. We don't just need to hear how much our partner loves us; we need to be able to feel it too.

Relationships can begin to fall apart when couples start to spend more and more time apart from one another doing their own thing. Different hobbies, friends, and interests can all lead to a divide. If there is a good balance, it can be perfectly healthy. However, if either one is spending vast amounts of time away with very little quality time spent with their partner, it won't be long before couples can drift apart from one another. If you notice that you no longer make time for one another, it is essential that you take time out to do something together that you can both enjoy. It can be something as simple as watching a movie together with no disruptions, or choosing a sport or activity to practise together. It doesn't matter what it is you choose; just be sure that you keep it up regularly to connect with each other as often as possible.

If you find that every little thing your partner does deeply irritates you, this is another clue that things may be on a downward spiral. If it gets to the stage in your relationship where either one, or even both of you, get annoyed constantly, it is definitely time to take a deeper look at the reasons why. Try to see that quite often these are habits that have been repeated over and again, possibly throughout the whole of their life, so complaining and nagging may make no difference whatsoever. All it will do is antagonise your partner who will feel that you are not happy and accepting of who they are, so trying to change them can cause further problems.

Realise that we all have our faults and weaknesses and that if we are in a committed relationship, especially when it is not going well, these faults will be highlighted and magnified. Learning to accept our partner for who they are and unconditionally loving them will allow us to be much more tolerant of irritating and annoying behaviours. When we take a look at ourselves in the mirror and see that we are not completely perfect, it will help us to look at our partner in a fairer and more rational way. No one is perfect and we shouldn't expect perfection from ourselves or from others. Think of all the positive qualities whenever we focus on the negative and work out ways together to overcome the irritating parts. You can make a list together of things you would like to try to change and then choose one or two to work on at a time. By looking at things in a more positive way rather than criticising and putting each other down, you should be able to reduce the frustration of bad habits and annoying ways much quicker.

If either partner feels incredibly insecure within the relationship, this can be a huge cause for concern. Insecurity can be due to low self-esteem, but it can also be because they do not feel secure and confident of the other person's feelings or intentions. If either partner feels as though they cannot totally be themselves with the other person, they will withdraw slightly and fear and doubt will creep in. This can be because they do not feel confident that they are accepted for who they are and may be judged and criticised by their partner. It is vital that to have a successful and loving relationship you can feel comfortable with each other and feel that you accept and appreciate each other for who you are. You both need to be able to talk freely and openly with each other without feeling that you are treading on eggshells or that something you say will offend the other person. If you are respectful and loving to one another, communication should flow naturally without one or the other person taking things too personally or being oversensitive unnecessarily.

Discussing your relationship in a negative light with friends, family, or colleagues is another sign that there is trouble ahead. Whilst it is natural that you want to talk through a problem that you may be facing with someone you can trust, badmouthing your partner on a regular basis to anyone that wants to listen is disrespectful. When you find that you are feeling the need to criticise your partner and complain about them to others, it is advisable to think carefully about whom you choose to talk to. Discussing these problems with close family can lead them to feel judgemental about your partner and your relationship. It can be difficult to get an honest opinion from someone close to you as they will most often be biased towards you and may feel differently towards your partner after they have heard your version of things. They will almost certainly take your side as they have only heard your side of the story and therefore may judge harshly giving you advice that is not balanced or possibly even relative to the actual reality of what has happened.

If you begin to notice that this is something that is happening more frequently and you are not getting any resolve, it is time to realise that work needs to be done within the relationship to get to the bottom of the problem rather than communicating it to others. Working things through together with your partner is almost always the most successful way of solving any problems that you come across. You will be able to both air exactly how you think and feel about the situation and should be able to talk things through fully until you come to an understanding that hopefully suits you both. Whilst we all need a friend or someone we can turn to for a shoulder to cry on, ultimately we should be able to turn to our partner to sort out relationship difficulties, or in certain cases it can also help to seek professional advice or counselling. It is important also to know that you shouldn't feel the need to cover up abusive behaviour. It is simply thinking about who you speak to and what you should say before you lay your relationship bare for all to see. Carefully selecting who we turn to in these times of need will prevent any unfair or biased opinions being created about your partner, which can be difficult to remove once formed.

Accept that from time to time all relationships will go through struggles. There may be times when you will feel that feelings have died down or there is too much water under the bridge for the relationship to continue. This is perfectly natural as negotiating a partnership together will at times be extremely testing and can make you feel like giving up when things become too difficult or emotions have fizzled away. When you go through a phase like this, before giving up and feeling that you have reached the end, have a good think about what you want from each other and for your future. Take a look at what has happened in the past and whether you think it is possible to build on what you have to turn things around and make things work.

Before walking away, consider if it is possible for you both to put the past behind you and learn from your mistakes, using the obstacles as learning curves to make you stronger together rather than pulling you apart. Just because there are disagreements and conflicts does not mean that you are not meant to be together. Use these as opportunities to improve communication and understand each other better so that they are not repeated again in the future. As long as you are always finding resolution and compromise together, there is always a chance that the relationship will work and be positive, regardless of how many disputes you may have. Speaking to one another in a respectful and caring manner rather than being bitter and angry when communicating will help to reach a conclusion much quicker with less turbulence.

Think about your partner in a logical manner casting all emotions aside. If you met your partner today, would you still be physically and sexually attracted to them? Are you still interested in them as a person? Do they have the same desires for the future as you do? Do you trust this person and can you depend on them? Are you together out of habit or from a genuine desire to spend your life with one another? Is the relationship abusive or destructive in any way? These types of questions need serious thought when considering if you are compatible with the other person and whether you are capable of having a fulfilling and long-lasting partnership.

If you have differences that are irreconcilable, making the decision to break up can be traumatic and painful. However, it is much better to assess the differences and properly think about what you want and what you get from the relationship rather than dragging the relationship out due to the fear of separation. Staying in a turbulent relationship or one that is no longer ticking the boxes can be much more damaging and hurtful than walking away and going through the stages of breaking up.

If you do not feel ready to break up but have reached a stage where you feel you need some time out, then you could suggest having a break or some space from each other. Be careful about how you bring the topic up because not everyone feels the same way about having a break. Some will not feel that it is the right path to take and that there are other options to explore before having time apart. Before making this decision, talk it through fully with your partner to ensure that the conditions of the break are mutually agreeable. Instead of feeling that your relationship has temporarily been put on hold so you are both free to do what you want with other people, try to see it as some time to yourself to think things through and reflect on what you want and need from each other. Understand that you may not both want to have the break. One person may feel the need for space whilst the other wants to work things through together, so finding a solution that suits you both is the only way to get through this. Otherwise, resentment, mistrust, and negative feelings may surface.

Use the time away from one another to get to know yourself again and to do some of the things you have been meaning to do that you enjoy and that you have not had the time to do recently. Sometimes we can get so intensely involved with the other person and the overall relationship that we lose ourselves and forget to do the things that make us happy. Having some time apart can help you to discover these things again and keeping up your own hobbies or interests once back together can make for a better balance within the relationship.

If you do decide to have time apart, agree beforehand on how much communication you would both like and what is and what isn't acceptable behaviour while you are apart. Acting like either of you are single again, while on an agreed break, is just going to add further problems to an already suffering relationship. Think carefully about why you want the break and do not use it as a way of letting the other person down gently. If either of you has already decided that the relationship has come to an end, communicate honestly so that you are both aware of where things are heading.

If you do not feel that a break will help matters, then think through other options. Couples can go to therapy, together or on their own. Choose reading material that may help or give you advice with resolving problems. Or, rather than taking a break from the relationship, just simply have a day away or a night away from each other to do something entirely on your own that you have wanted to do for a while. It can be as simple as spending quality time with a family member or booking into a tranquil hotel by the sea and relaxing for the day. Having a little space can just give you enough breathing space to clear your mind and feel refreshed to deal with what is going wrong in the relationship. It may be quite the opposite and you need to set aside some time together for quality time if this has been lacking lately. Doing something new together or getting away from everyday life for a short while can sometimes be just what is needed to help you connect with one another again.

If you can recognise what the problems and issues are, write down how you feel and work out an action plan that is manageable to resolve things together. When there is something that you find reoccurs, causing you to fight with one another, talk through ways of resolving it so that in the future you can avoid getting into conflict over it. Sometimes it can be something really simple that can be put into place to stop continuous bickering over trivial matters that soon develop into more heated arguments. Don't ignore problems. Taking note of what is wrong and working out compromises and resolving issues together is what sets the basis for a strong and lasting relationship.

Apologising and Forgiveness

'Love means never having to say you are sorry.' is a quote from the 1970 movie Love Story. It has different meanings for different people and is possibly one of the most controversial and discussed quotes from a romantic film. Some people see it as that if you love someone, you will act accordingly and never do anything to hurt that person. But in reality, this is quite impossible. We are all different and whether intended or not, we will at some point do something within a relationship for which an apology is required. Some people see the quote as meaning that you do not need your partner to apologise, because, if you love each other, you will understand that you would not have intentionally done anything to cause pain, therefore, never needing to say sorry.

However you see the quote or whatever you take from it, it is not difficult to see that at times we all need to admit when we have gone wrong and let our partners know that we regret our actions. Whether it is about uttering the words 'I'm sorry' or taking the time to let your partner know that you are aware that your behaviour was not acceptable, it is important to recognise when you need to acknowledge this.

In every relationship, there comes a time when you need to apologise or forgive, or even both at the same time. Both of these words can so easily be misused and misunderstood, so by looking at both things a little closer it can help us to resolve issues easier by having a greater understanding of how we are acting and reacting when the situation arises.

Ego plays one of the biggest parts in being able to apologise. Our pride and ego get in the way and can prevent us from admitting when we are wrong. We need to see that our relationship is much more important than our ego and we will do serious damage to it, often irreparable, if we do not let go of our ego and admit when we have made a mistake.

Timing is relevant when you need to apologise. Leaving things for too long when you have done something wrong can lead to built-up resentment and can cause more pain. We can also have selective memories and after a period of time our memories can become misconstrued and can make it more difficult to see how the other person is feeling. The quicker you can accept responsibility and admit where you have gone wrong, the more chance you have at rectifying things and seeing things from the other person's perspective.

There is quite a lot to learn about apologising and forgiveness. Unfortunately, it is never quite as simple as just saying the words. Too many times the word is used lightly to achieve 'quick forgiveness' or to avoid confrontation. Often, people feel that it is OK to behave badly because as long as they say sorry, all will be forgiven and this gives them free reign to act however they want and make things OK again.

For it to be sincere, there has to be meaning and depth behind what you are saying; otherwise, they are empty words, and quite often the other person will be able to pick up on this. If you feel that your partner is the one in the wrong, but you are getting the blame, there can be a lot of pressure to back down and it may feel easier to say sorry just so there is no tension. However, this is not always the best option, so try to explain how you are feeling to the other person and that you do not see that you have done anything wrong. Listen to what they say in response and it will give you a greater understanding of how they feel and you may find a mutually agreeable way of resolving things.

At times you may say or do something unintentionally that causes the other person some distress. In these cases, it will not hurt to say that you are sorry your actions have caused them to feel this way, but make it clear that you did not set out to do this. However, you validate how they feel and will do your best to avoid this happening again in the future.

To be authentic when apologising, you need to first of all accept some responsibility for the part you have played. Try not to make any excuse for the way you have acted or pass on blame to the other person. If we want someone to forgive us, we have to accept and make them see that we are aware that our behaviour was unacceptable and we are willing to make changes to prevent it from happening again. When we are feeling hurt and angry, it can be very difficult to admit to ourselves, let alone others, that we have made a mistake. When we accept that we are in the wrong and want to rectify the situation, an apology will go some way towards letting the other person know that you regret the way you have behaved.

However, this does not mean that the other person will automatically accept this apology. We have to be aware that everyone deals with things differently and while one person may be ready to take a step towards making up, the other may not be ready to do this quite yet. In some cases, the other person may not ever want to reconcile. Just because the other person may not be willing to accept your apology at this stage, does not mean that it should not have been offered. When possible, you should always try to be honest with yourself and others and if you are aware that you have done something that requires an apology, you should let the other person know that you are sorry and regret your actions. When they have calmed down, they may see things differently and it is not very often that apologies go unappreciated.

It may be that you need to give the other person a little space and time to come around. If this is the case, let them know that you are sorry and are waiting for when they are ready to talk to you. Have some patience and don't expect too much from them; you have hurt their feelings and they may require space to think things through. Don't storm out and get angry if they are not ready to make up when you are. This will just fuel things even further. Let them know that you understand that what you have done has hurt their feelings and that you are sorry for your behaviour and will be waiting for when they are ready to communicate with you. Hopefully, it won't take long for them to realise that you are asking for their forgiveness and to be open to listening to you to help build bridges.

There will be times when more than one person is at fault. This can bring out stubbornness and may make you feel like withholding the apology until the other person admits that they are at fault. A stand-off can occur with both partners equally unwilling to make the first move to repair and resolve the situation. It will take the strength of character of one person to come forward and make the first move. Just because you are the first to apologise does not mean that you have to take full responsibility for everything that has happened or that the other person is less guilty. Make it clear that you are completely aware of where you went wrong and want to admit to your fault and rectify things and then let them know how you feel about the way that they have acted.

Hopefully, the other person will then admit to the part they have played and will also offer a sincere apology. Understand, though, that two people will never see things exactly the same way, so although you may feel hurt by someone's actions, it does not mean that they will also perceive things this way. Letting each other know how you feel is the only way to gain a clearer perception of how your partner is feeling, so do your best to calmly and honestly talk things through so you can try to clear the air.

Saying that you are sorry is not the only way to let a person know how you feel. You can use various ways to let them know that you regret what you have done. While buying flowers or chocolates are still acts of thoughtfulness, doing something more heartfelt can really help to get the message across. Writing a letter, booking a nice cosy meal somewhere or cooking for them, making a sentimental gift, or arranging to spend time doing something together you know they will really enjoy are all ways that you can show how you are feeling. Ask your partner if there is anything they would like you to do together and, if possible, make the arrangements for them. There are so many different things you can do to let someone know that you care for them, so think of something unique to the two of you and do whatever it takes to let the other person know that you care and want to try to put things right.

Forgiving someone can benefit you much more than it can the other person. One of the main reasons that it is important to forgive is because we cannot truly judge anyone's behaviour. We are all very different and complex individuals that have each had our own set of conditioning and beliefs. We will not all think or act the same way, and we will never totally understand how or why another person behaves the way they did. By having compassion and humility, we can try to detach from the pain of their actions and find our own way of coming to terms with what has happened.

If we do not forgive, the anger and pain connected to it will eat away at us from the inside out. It can become unbearable and we can become so immersed in hatred that it can cause us to feel physically and emotionally unwell. When we release these feelings, we will instantly feel better and find it easier to let go of the painful memories associated to the memory.

Just because we forgive, it does not mean that we are accepting the behaviour or that we are willing to forget what has happened. Forgiving is saying that you are not going to hold on to the negativity of the situation and that you are going to accept in your mind that you no longer wish to harbour bitter feelings and resentments for the way you are feeling or towards the person that has done something to cause this pain. Once you have made that decision, you can work on ways to overcome the emotions you are feeling and replace the destructive feelings with more positive and loving ones.

Forgiveness is not about suddenly forgetting what has gone wrong and excusing or brushing the behaviour under the carpet. In order that we do not continue to allow people to treat us this way in the future, we must not only make it clear that what has happened is unacceptable but also make our feelings clear so that the other person is aware of our boundaries. Forgiving does not mean that you have to reconcile the relationship or put yourself in a position where this could happen again. It is about releasing yourself from the painful feelings and not letting the emotions control you so that you can be free from the impact of the negative behaviour of the other person.

Choosing to reconcile with your partner is entirely different from choosing forgiveness. While we can forgive our partner, it may not mean that we still want to be in a relationship with them. Each person's tolerance levels are different and what one person can get over within a relationship, another person cannot.

We need to set ourselves clear boundaries so that we are treated respectfully, and we should make our partner aware of what is and what is not acceptable. If they cross the line, we may choose to give them another chance or even many more chances in some cases. This is a personal choice and while it can be very damaging to your self-esteem to regularly be treated badly, each individual is responsible for whether they choose to stay or go.

Now

Living in the here and now is the only way to ever experience true happiness. When we are in a relationship and there are problems, we can focus too much on the past or the future and forget about the now. Now is the only time that you are going to experience true emotion. Looking forward or back in time will only either conjure up false illusions of the past and future or your selective memory will create a deluded image instead of seeing the reality.

The most important thing of all is not to let the past threaten the present moment. Live for now! Enjoy every moment spent with your partner. To begin to have an enriching relationship with your partner in the present moment, you must first learn how to appreciate living in the now. When we live in the now, we can achieve so much more and the benefits for our well-being and relationship are vast. We can truly connect with the reality of life rather than perceiving how things were before or what will happen ahead. When we can engage with what is happening in the moment, we can experience real joy and emotions that aren't fuelled by fear, worries, and regret.

It will take a little practice to live in the present moment and there will be many times when your mind will skip forward or back. When this happens, just trigger your thoughts to remind yourself to discard those thoughts and relax in the now. Become aware of how you are feeling and how it feels to be living without projecting any thoughts from the past or future.

We can miss out on so much by not being aware of what is happening in the present moment and enjoying it. Sometimes we are so busy trying to multitask, juggling all of life's demands, that we fail to notice really important things that are happening right before us. Our minds are so full of nonsense that we find it hard to process the simplest of details and this can cause life to pass us by without having a great deal of meaning to it.

The only thing that is real and accessible is now. It is also the only thing we have any control over. The past has already gone and the future is not yet here, so we have to make the most of what we have, which is this moment now. We can never live in the past or the future, so there is no point allowing our mind to live there. Worrying about things that have happened or things that we fear will happen in the future causes distress and anxiety and prevents us from living in the moment. Just becoming consciously aware of the thoughts that are in our mind is a great way to begin to live in the present moment. As we take notice of our thoughts, we can discard the ones that are negative and are not connected to the present and instead pay attention to how it feels right now instead.

When we are aware of how we are feeling in the present moment without the addition of the stress and strain brought on from negative thinking, we can enjoy the time spent with our partners and those around us. If we are too busy thinking about what happened in the past or what we think is going to happen in the future, we are going to completely miss out on what is happening now. This means we are wasting valuable moments of our life that could be spent enjoying our partner's company.

When we are in a relationship, we make commitments to one another such as marriage, living together, and having a family together and we hope these things will last forever. We desperately want to be with this person forever and this can cause us to feel fearful and to worry that it may not last. If we live in the moment, we can enjoy what is happening right now instead of thinking about something we do not have very much control over. If we are loving and happy and enjoy the present moment, we will be much better company for our partner and make them more interested in staying around, rather than being full of anxiety and worry.

If we are reliving negative thoughts related to our partner's past, all we are doing is recreating the deluded perceptions that we have built up in our head. We continually recreate painful and destructive scenarios, when instead we should be concentrating on what is happening now as that is the only thing that is of any importance.

We can lose so much of life's experiencing by not being aware of the present moment. By recognising when our mind is jumping to the past or the future and slowly bringing it back to the present moment, we can learn to avoid what Buddhists call the monkey mind—the constant chatter in our minds that prevents us from truly relaxing in the moment. Simply concentrating on our breathing and letting go of any thoughts that are not connected to the moment are easy ways to bring the mind back to the here and now.

When our lives are very routine, it is much easier to switch to autopilot and go through the day without paying attention to anything that is going on around us, including our partners, which can cause us to take everything for granted and not appreciate what we have.

We must take care to appreciate the present moment as it is the only moment we will ever have. The ones in the past have gone and the future ones are not yet here.

Being in the present moment is also beneficial for emotional awareness. When we are focused on what is happening now, we can feel the reality of the emotions connected to it. Sometimes this may be uncomfortable when we are going through particularly stressful or painful times, but it is much better to be fully present and aware so that we can deal with things with a clear and focused mind.

We can from time to time reflect on the past so that we can avoid making repeated mistakes and also enjoy reliving precious moments. Also, we should take time to think of our future and make plans so that we can reach our goals and ambitions. However, when we have this time set aside, we should do it constructively, so it does not affect our enjoyment of the present moment and prevent us from experiencing the pleasure of a loving, romantic relationship.

When we are not fully in the present moment, our ego can take over, telling us we are not good enough or too good or basically anything other than what we actually are. The ego creates a false persona and the only way to have any control over this is to be in the present moment and aware of who we are and what we are feeling. By doing this, we have a greater sense of what is going on around us and can more clearly see the relationships we have and gain a better insight into any problems that need working on.

In understanding more about the ego, we must realise that although we need to work out ways to override the ego so that it does not take over the majority of our thoughts and actions, we also need our ego to help us have rational minds to solve problems. Rather than turning against our ego, we just need to turn it down so that it does not cause us to think negatively about ourselves, our past, or our future. In doing this, we will become much more at peace with ourselves and our surroundings, which this will have a direct impact on intimate relationships.

To stop allowing the ego to control your thoughts, all you need to do is to keep aware and bring yourself back to the moment, and you will instantly have a clearer perspective on your surroundings. Every time you feel your mind drifting to the past or the future in a negative light or feel your ego attacking your self-esteem, just take a breath and let go of the thoughts, bringing your mind back to the present moment. It really is that simple and, with plenty of practice, will become easier and much more natural over time. One day, without even realising it, you will suddenly notice how you are living in the present moment the majority of the time and have much more control over every aspect of your life and, importantly, your relationship.

Made in the USA
Lexington, KY
16 April 2018